THE PIECE OF FIRE

by the same author

Folk Tales

THE HAT-SHAKING DANCE (Ghana)

THE TIGER'S WHISKER (Asia and the Pacific)

KANTCHIL'S LIME PIT (Indonesia)

THE COW-TAIL SWITCH (West Africa)
with George Herzog

THE FIRE ON THE MOUNTAIN (Ethiopia)
with Wolf Leslau

TERRAPIN'S POT OF SENSE (United States)

THE KING'S DRUM (Africa south of the Sahara)

RIDE WITH THE SUN (around the world)

UNCLE BOUQUI OF HAITI (Haiti)

Other

THE DRUM AND THE HOE—Life and Lore of the Haitian People

THE BIG OLD WORLD OF RICHARD CREEKS

THE CABALLERO

NEGRO FOLK MUSIC U.S.A.

SHAPING OUR TIMES—What the United Nations Is and Does

HAITI SINGING

ON RECOGNIZING THE HUMAN SPECIES

NEGRO SONGS FROM ALABAMA

The Piece of Fire

and Other Haitian Tales

Harold Courlander

Illustrated by Beth and Joe Krush

Harcourt, Brace & World, Inc., New York

First edition
Library of Congress Catalog Card Number: 64-12507
Printed in the United States of America

Contents

MERISIER, STRONGER THAN THE ELEPHANTS 9
THE CHIEF OF THE WELL 15
BOUKI GETS WHEE-AI 20
BREAK MOUNTAINS 23
BOUKI RENTS A HORSE 25
PIERRE JEAN'S TORTOISE 29
THE CAT, THE DOG, AND DEATH 34
SWEET MISERY 37
THE GUN, THE POT, AND THE HAT 39
THE LIZARD'S BIG DANCE 50
BOUKI BUYS A BURRO 55
TICOUMBA AND THE PRESIDENT 58
NANANBOUCLOU AND THE PIECE OF FIRE 62
THE FISHERMEN 64
WHO IS THE OLDER? 70
THE VOYAGE BELOW THE WATER 71
BOUKI CUTS WOOD 76
THE DONKEY DRIVER 81
THE BLACKSMITHS 84
BOUKI'S GLASSES 89
CHARLES LEGOUN AND HIS FRIEND 91
BOUKI AND TI BEF 94

THE KING OF THE ANIMALS 97
JANOT COOKS FOR THE EMPEROR 101
JEAN BRITISSE, THE CHAMPION 105
WAITING FOR A TURKEY 111
SOME COMMENTS ON HAITIAN FOLK TALES 113
NOTES ON THE STORIES 118

Merisier, Stronger Than the Elephants

THERE was an old man with three sons. One day he fell ill, and he sent a message to his sons, asking them to come to his house. When they arrived, he said to them, "I am an old man, I am sick. If I should die, how will you bury me?"

One son answered, "Father, may you grow strong again. But if you should die, I would have you buried in a mahogany coffin."

Another son answered, "Father, may you live long. But if you should die, I would make you a coffin of brass."

And the third son, named Brisé, replied, "Father, I would bury you in the great drum of the king of the elephants."

"The great drum of the king of the elephants! Who before now has ever been buried so magnificiently!" the old man said. "Yes, that is the way it should be." And he asked the son who had suggested it to bring him the drum of the king of the elephants.

Brisé went home. He told his wife: "I said I would do this thing for my father, but it is impossible. Why didn't I say

I would make him a coffin of silver? Even that would have been more possible. How shall I ever be able to do what I have promised?"

His wife prepared food for him and gave him his knapsack. Brisé began his journey. But he didn't know where to find the elephants. He asked here, he asked there, but no one knew where the elephants were to be found. As evening came on, he met a blind beggar who was being led by a small boy. The beggar said, "Man, give me a little of whatever you have, a piece of bread or a taste of rice."

Brisé took a piece of cornbread from his pocket and gave it to the beggar. "If you were not blind," he said, "I would ask you if you had ever seen the elephants."

"Even men with eyes have not seen the elephants," the beggar answered.

Brisé went on. When it was dark, he slept in the grass by the edge of the road. When day came, he walked again, asking everywhere for information about the elephants.

When the sun became hot, Brisé went to sit in the shade of a large tree. There, sitting on a stone, he saw a crippled man with only one foot and a crutch. "Give me a little of what you have in your knapsack," the man said. "I have a great hunger in my stomach."

Brisé gave him a piece of cornbread. They talked. Brisé said, "I have two feet, while you have only one. You go slowly, and I travel far. But what good is that when I don't know where to find the great drum of the king of the elephants?"

He continued on his way. And as night came on, he saw an old man sitting before a little fire at the edge of the road. The old man said, "Come and rest here."

Brisé sat down and opened his knapsack. There were

only two pieces of cornbread left. He gave one to the old man and ate the other one himself. After a while the old man said: "I thank you for the third piece of cornbread, which I have just finished. I thank you for the second piece. I thank you for the first piece."

Brisé said, "Papa, you are mistaken. I gave you only one."

The old man said, "No, it is you who are mistaken. At noon I was a man with one foot and a crutch, and yesterday I was a blind beggar. My name is Merisier."

Then Brisé understood that the old man was a *houngan*, a Vodoun priest with magical powers. The old man took out his bead-covered rattle. He shook it and went into a trance and talked with the gods. At last he put the rattle away and said: "Go that way, to the north, across the grassland. There is a great *mapou* tree, called *Mapou Plus Grand Passé Tout*. Wait there. The elephants come there with the drum. They dance until they are tired, then they fall asleep. When they sleep, take the drum. Travel fast. Here are four wari nuts for protection. If you are pursued, throw a wari nut behind you and say, 'Merisier is stronger than the elephants.' "

When day came, Brisé went north across the grasslands. He came to the tree called *Mapou Plus Grand Passé Tout*. He climbed into the tree and waited. As the sun was going down, he saw a herd of elephants coming, led by their king. They gathered around the *mapou* tree. The king's drummer began to play on the great drum. The elephants began to dance. The ground shook with their stamping. The dancing went on and on, all night. They danced until the first cocks began to crow. Then they stopped, lay down on the ground, and slept.

Brisé came down from the tree. He was in the middle of a large circle of elephants. He took the great drum and placed it on his head. He climbed first over one sleeping elephant, then another, until he was outside the circle. He traveled as fast as he could with his heavy load.

When he was halfway across the grassland, he heard the enraged elephant herd coming after him. When they were very close, he took one of the wari nuts the old man had given him and threw it behind him, saying, "Merisier is stronger than the elephants!" And where the nut fell, a tremendous pine forest grew up instantly. The elephants stopped running and began to work their way slowly through the trees. Brisé went on.

He walked a great distance. Again he heard the sound of the elephants coming. He took another wari nut and

threw it behind him, saying, "Merisier is stronger than the elephants!" And where the nut fell, there was suddenly a large fresh-water lake. The elephants stopped at its shore.

The king of the elephants commanded, "Drink up the water, so that we can pass!" The elephants began drinking, and slowly, very slowly, the level of the lake went down.

Brisé traveled far. He was almost across the grassland. He heard the elephants coming again. He threw a third wari nut on the ground behind him, saying, "Merisier is stronger than the elephants!" This time there appeared a large salt-water lake.

The king of the elephants commanded, "Drink it up so that we can pass!" The elephants began drinking. The salt water made them sick. But their king commanded, "Drink, drink!" So they continued to drink, and one by

one they fell dying. Only the king of the elephants did not drink, and at last he alone of the herd was alive.

Brisé came out of the grassland. He followed the trails. He went to his father's house with the drum. When he arrived, his father was not dead; he was not sick; he was working with his hoe in the fields.

"Put the drum away," the father said. "I don't need it yet. I am feeling fine."

Brisé took the drum to his own house. He ate and slept. When he awoke, he heard a loud noise in the courtyard. He saw the king of elephants coming. The elephant ran straight toward the great drum and seized hold of it.

Brisé took the last wari nut that the Vodoun priest had given him and threw it on the ground, saying, "Merisier is stronger than the elephants!"

Instantly the great drum broke into small pieces, and each piece became a small drum. The king of elephants broke into many pieces, and each piece became a drummer. The drummers went everywhere, each one taking a drum with him.

Thus it is that there are drums everywhere in the country. Thus it is that people have a proverb which says: "Every drum has a drummer."

And thus it is, also, that no one has ever been buried in a drum.

The Chief of the Well

There was once a drought in the country. The streams dried up and the wells went dry, and there was no place for the animals to get water. The animals met to discuss the situation—the cow, the dog, the goat, the horse, the donkey, and all the others. They decided to ask God for help. Together they went to God and told him how bad things were. God thought, then he said, "Don't bother your heads. They don't call me God for nothing. I will give you one well for everyone to use."

The animals thanked God. They said he was very considerate. God said, "But you will have to take good care of it. One of you will have to be the caretaker. He will stay by the well at all times to see that no one abuses it or makes it dirty."

Mabouya the ground lizard spoke up, saying, "I will be caretaker."

God looked at all the animals. He said at last, "Mabouya the lizard looks like the best caretaker. Therefore, I appoint him. He will be the watchman. The well is over there in that mango grove."

The animals went away. The lizard went directly to the well. When the other animals began to come for water, Mabouya challenged them. First the cow came to drink, and the lizard sang out in a deep voice:

> "Who is it? Who is it?
> Who is walking in my grove?"

The cow replied:

> "It is I, the cow.
> I am coming for water."

And the lizard called back:

> "Go away, this is God's grove,
> And the well is dry."

So the cow went away and suffered from thirst.

Then the horse came, and the lizard challenged him, saying:

> "Who is it? Who is it?
> Who is walking in my grove?"

The horse answered:

> "It is I, the horse.
> I am coming for water."

And the lizard called back:

> "Go away, this is God's grove,
> And the well is dry."

So the horse went away, and he too suffered from thirst.

Each animal came to the well, and the lizard challenged all of them in the same way, saying:

> "Go away, this is God's grove,
> And the well is dry."

So the animals went away and suffered much because they had no water to drink.

When God saw all the suffering going on, he said: "I gave the animals a well to drink from, but they are all dying of thirst. What is the matter?" And he himself went to the well. When the lizard heard his footsteps, he called out:

"Who is it? Who is it?
Who is walking in my grove?"

God answered:

"It is I, Papa God.
I am coming for water."

And the lizard said:

"Go away, Papa God.
The well is dry."

God was very angry. He said once more:

"It is I, Papa God.
I am coming for water."

And the lizard called back to him again:

"Go away, Papa God.
The well is dry."

God said no more to the lizard. He sent for the other animals to come to the well. He said: "You came to me because you were thirsty, and I gave you a well. I made Mabouya the caretaker. But he thought the well was his. He became conceited. He gave no thought to the suffering creatures all around him. If a man has a banana tree in his garden, it is his. If a man has a cotton tree in his garden, it

is his. But if a man has a well in his garden, only the hole in the ground belongs to him. The water is God's and belongs to all creatures. Because Mabouya the lizard became drunk with conceit, he is no longer the caretaker. Henceforth, he must drink his water from puddles where-ever the rain falls. The new caretaker will be the frog. And the frog will not say, "Go away, the well is dry." He will say, "This is God's well, this is God's well."

So the animals drank at the well, while Mabouya the lizard went away from it and drank rain water wherever he could find it. The frog is now the caretaker. And all night he calls out:

"This is God's well!
This is God's well!
This is God's well!"

And it is a saying among the people:

"The hole in the ground is yours, the water is God's."

Bouki Gets Whee-ai

ONE day a country man named Bouki went to the city to sell some of his yams. He wandered through the market looking at the things that people were selling there—plantains, rice, beans, and pineapples. If he came to a place where a woman was selling little cakes, he would stand there looking and sniffing. His appetite increased.

He saw an old man sitting on his heels near the edge of the market. The old man was eating something. He was enjoying it tremendously. Bouki's mouth began to water. He tipped his hat politely to the old man and said, "Where can I get some of whatever you are eating?"

But the old man was deaf. He didn't hear a word that Bouki said. He only smiled and nodded his head.

So Bouki said again, "Excuse me, what is the name of that wonderful food you are eating?"

Just at that moment the old man bit into a hot pepper. It burned his tongue, and he cried out, "Whee-ai!"

"Thank you," Bouki said. "Thank you kindly."

He went through the market, asking everywhere, "Can I get some whee-ai here?"

No one had any whee-ai. Everyone laughed.

On his way home Bouki stopped along the road wherever vendors were selling food and asked for five centimes' worth of whee-ai. People just shook their heads, or they put their hands over their mouths to keep from laughing.

Bouki became cross. When he reached home, he asked Madame Bouki to make him some whee-ai. She laughed. He asked the neighbors, and they also laughed. Bouki told his son Tijean to go out and find some whee-ai for him. Tijean went from one place to another asking for five centimes' worth of whee-ai. He asked until he was tired of asking and sat down by the edge of the trail to rest.

Bouki's friend Ti Malice came along. He asked, "What is the matter?" Tijean told him about the whee-ai. Ti Malice sat down too and thought for a long time. Then he said, "I can get Bouki his whee-ai. Come to my place with me."

At Ti Malice's house, Ti Malice took a sack, and he put some thorny cactus leaves in the bottom. He put some oranges into the sack. He put a pineapple in. He put in a yam. He put in some potatoes. He closed the sack and gave it to Tijean. "There," Ti Malice said, "this is what Bouki is looking for."

Tijean took the sack home. He gave it to Bouki, saying, "I looked everywhere. I didn't find it, but Ti Malice found it. Here it is."

Bouki grabbed the sack. He put in his hand and took out a potato.

"That's no whee-ai!" he said.

He put his hand in again and took out a yam.

"That's no whee-ai!" he said with a frown.

He put his hand in again and took out a pineapple.

"That's not whee-ai!" he said crossly.

He put in his hand again and took out an orange.

"That's not whee-ai!"

He pushed his hand to the bottom of the sack and took hold of a thorny cactus leaf. The needles stuck into his fingers.

"Whee-ai!" he shouted in pain. "Whee-ai! Whee-ai!"

The neighbors came running. "What's the matter? What is happening?" they asked.

Tijean jumped up and down and clapped his hands.

"Nothing's the matter," he told them. "Papa's just happy. He's got his whee-ai."

Break Mountains

WHEN he was just born, Break Mountains was restless. He said to his mother, "When are you going to stop carrying me around as though I am a child? Put me down." She set him down. He said, "Why is the door always closed?" And he pulled the door off its hinges and threw it out of the house. "The mosquitoes will come in," his mother said. Break Mountains went out and pulled up an orange tree by the roots and fanned the air with it to drive the mosquitoes away. The wind he made put out the fire over which the dinner was cooking. So he ate his food raw. He said, "Let us dance." He hit his father's drum, and it broke into pieces. He became angry and pulled out the foundation poles of the house. The house fell down.

A hawk flew by. "Go away, there is nothing for you here," Break Mountains said. He reached for something to throw. A goat wandered by. Break Mountains picked up the goat, threw it, and knocked the hawk down.

"I have lived here all my life. Now I'm going to see something of the world," he said. He got on his father's donkey. The donkey fell down. He mounted his father's horse. The horse fell down. So he began walking. Each step he took was from the top of one hill to the top of the next, and every hill he stepped on became flattened out. He sneezed, and the wind knocked down a forest of pine trees. He stamped his foot and caused a landslide forty miles away. When he came to the lake called Etang Saumatre, he sat in it; the water rose up and flooded the canefields in the valley. A fisherman's boat sailed on the flood all the way to Gonaïves and landed in the desert.

Break Mountains went to the city. He said, "I need a pair of sandals." There was nothing big enough for him. They made a pair out of two whole cowhides, but they were too small. He went to the blacksmith and had sandals made out of iron. He put them on while the iron was still hot. He stepped into the ocean to cool off the sandals and made a wave that upset all the ships in the harbor.

"I am a hard fellow," Break Mountains said.

A bird flew overhead with a kernel of corn in its mouth. It dropped the seed, and the seed fell on Break Mountains' head. Break Mountains fell down. He couldn't get up. He said, "I want my mamma."

Bouki Rents a Horse

IT WAS time to dig up the yams and take them to market. Bouki went out with his big hoe and dug up a big pile of yams and left them in the sun to dry. While they were drying, he began to consider how he would get them to the city. "I think I will borrow Moussa's donkey," he said at last. "As long as I have the donkey, I might as well dig up some more yams."

So he dug up some more yams, and then he went to Moussa's house for the donkey. But Moussa said, "Bouki, my donkey ran away yesterday, and we haven't found him yet. "Why don't you rent a horse from Mr. Toussaint?"

"Toussaint!" Bouki said. "He'll charge more than I can get for the yams! He'll charge me even for *talking* to him!"

But finally Bouki went to Toussaint's house to see if he could rent a horse.

Toussaint said, "This is a good horse. He's too good to carry yams. But you can have him for one day for fifteen gourdes."

Bouki had only five gourdes.

"I'll take the five now," Toussaint said. "You can give me ten more tomorrow when you come for the horse."

Bouki went home. He went to sleep. In the morning when he got up to go to market, Moussa was in front of his house with the donkey.

"Here's the donkey," Moussa said. "He came home in the middle of the night."

Bouki said, "But I already rented Toussaint's horse!"

"Never mind, go tell Toussaint you don't need the horse," Moussa said.

"But I already gave him five gourdes," Bouki complained. "I'll never get my money back!"

Just then Ti Malice came along. He listened to the talk. He said, "Take me along to Toussaint's. I'll get your money back for you."

Bouki and Ti Malice went together to Toussaint's place.

"We've come for the horse," Ti Malice said.

"There he is under the tree," Toussaint said. "But first give me the ten gourdes."

"Not so fast," Ti Malice said. "First we have to see if he's big enough."

"He's big enough," Toussaint said. "He's the biggest horse around here. So give me the ten gourdes."

"First we have to measure him," Ti Malice said. He took a measuring tape from his pocket and stretched it over the horse's back. "Let's see, now," he said to Bouki. "You need about eighteen inches, and you can sit in the middle. I need about fifteen inches, and I can sit here. Madame Malice needs about eighteen inches, and she can sit behind me. Madame Bouki needs about twenty inches, and she can sit in the front."

"Wait!" Toussaint said. "You can't put four people on that horse!"

"Then," Ti Malice said, "Tijean Bouki can go here on the horse's neck. Boukino can sit in his lap, and we can tie Boukinette right here if we're careful."

"Listen!" Toussaint said, starting to sweat. "You must be crazy. A horse can't carry so many people!"

"He can try," Ti Malice said.

"You'll kill him!" Toussaint said.

"We can put my children *here*," Ti Malice said, measuring behind the horse's ears, "but they'll have to push together."

"Just a minute!" Toussaint shouted. "You can't have the horse at all!"

"Oh yes, we can," Ti Malice said, still measuring. "You

rented him to us, and today we are going to use him. Bouki, where will we put the baby?"

"Baby?" Bouki said. "Baby?"

"We'll put the baby here," Ti Malice said. "Madame Bouki can hold him. Then over here we can hang the saddle bags to carry the pigs."

"The deal is off!" Toussaint shouted. "This animal isn't a steamship!"

"Now don't try to back out of the deal," Ti Malice said, "or we'll take the matter to the police."

"Here!" Toussaint said. "Here's your five gourdes back!"

"Five gourdes!" Ti Malice said. "You rented him to us for *fifteen*, and now you want to give *five* back? What do you take us for?"

"Yes," Bouki said, "what for?"

"But Bouki only *gave* me five!" Toussaint said.

Ti Malice looked the horse over carefully.

"Where will we put Grandmother?" Bouki asked suddenly.

"Here!" Toussaint shouted. "Here!" He pushed fifteen gourdes into Ti Malice's hands. "And get away from my horse!" He jumped on its back and rode away.

Bouki and Ti Malice watched him go. Then they fell on the ground and began to laugh. They laughed so hard that they had to gasp for air.

Suddenly Bouki stopped laughing. He looked worried. He sat up.

"What's the matter?" Ti Malice asked.

"I don't think we could have done it," Bouki said.

"Done what?" Ti Malice asked.

"Put Grandmother on the horse," Bouki said.

Pierre Jean's Tortoise

A TORTOISE was crawling along slowly one day when he came to a garden where many birds were eating. It was the garden of a farmer named Pierre Jean. The turkey, the chicken, the pigeon, the duck, the gris-gris bird, and all the others were there. They invited the tortoise to eat with them. But the tortoise said, "Oh, no. If the farmer who owns this garden should surprise us, you would fly away. But where would I be? He would catch me and beat me."

The birds said, "Don't bother your head about that. We will give you feathers. Then you too can fly." Each of the birds took out some of its feathers and attached them to tortoise, until he looked more like a bird than anything else. So he came and ate with them.

But while they were eating, one of the birds called out: "The farmer is coming! The farmer is coming!" The birds quickly grabbed the feathers they had given the tortoise. They flew away. Tortoise crawled, crawled, crawled, but he was too slow. Pierre Jean, the farmer, caught him. Pierre Jean was about to beat him for eating up his garden, but the tortoise began to sing:

"Colico Pierre Jean oh!
Colico Pierre Jean oh!
If I could I would fly, *enhé!*
What a tragedy, I have no wings!"

The farmer was amazed to hear the tortoise sing. He asked him to sing again. The tortoise sang in his best voice.

"What a curious thing," Pierre Jean said. "Who ever heard of a singing tortoise?" He took the tortoise home and put him in a box, which he then placed in the rafters for safe keeping. Then he went down to the city. In the marketplace he found a crowd, and he said: "Who ever heard of a singing tortoise?"

The people answered: "There is no such thing."

Pierre Jean took money from his pocket. He said: "Who will bet there is no such thing as a singing tortoise?" Some men bet this, some men bet that. There was much excitement.

While they were talking this way, the President came along in his carriage. He stopped and called out, "What is going on?"

When he heard about Pierre Jean's singing tortoise, the President said: "This man is a mischief maker. Tortoises don't sing. I will bet one hundred thousand gourdes there is no such thing as a singing tortoise."

But Pierre Jean replied: "My President, I am a poor farmer. Where would I ever get a hundred thousand gourdes?"

The President said: "Pierre Jean, you are a rascal. You are trying to make mischief. I will bet the hundred thou-

sand gourdes. If a tortoise talks, I will pay you. But if a tortoise doesn't talk, I will have you shot."

This was the way it was in the marketplace. But back in the country Pierre Jean's wife heard that her husband had a singing tortoise. So she searched the house until she found him. She asked him to sing.

"I can sing only by the edge of the river," the tortoise told her. So she took him to the edge of the river.

"My feet must be wet," the tortoise said. So she placed him in the water by the riverbank. And before she knew what was happening, the tortoise slid into the river and swam away.

Madame Pierre Jean heard the crowd coming up the trail from the marketplace. She was frightened. Her husband's tortoise was gone. She ran home, and on the way she caught a small lizard. She put the lizard in the box where the tortoise had been and closed the lid. When the crowd from the city arrived, Pierre Jean took them to the box. The President said: "Let the singing begin."

Pierre Jean called out, "Sing, tortoise!"

The lizard replied from inside the box: "Crik!"

Pierre Jean called again, "Sing tortoise, sing!"

And the lizard replied: "Crak!"

The President was angry. He said: "You call that singing? Open the box!" They opened the box. They saw only the small lizard.

The President said: "This man is a vagabond! He thinks we are stupid! Take him down to the river and have him shot!"

So they took Pierre Jean down to the riverbank and stood him against a tree to shoot him. Just at this moment the tortoise stuck his head out of the water and sang:

"Colico Pierre Jean oh!
Colico Pierre Jean oh!
If you could you would fly, *enhé!*
What a tragedy, you have no wings!"

"Ah! That is my tortoise!" Pierre Jean said. "Listen to him sing!"

And the tortoise sang again:
"Colico, oh President!
Colico, oh President!
Uncle Pierre Jean talks too much, *enhé!*
Stupidity doesn't kill a man, but it makes him sweat!"

When the President heard that, he laughed. He freed Pierre Jean and paid him the hundred thousand gourdes. The tortoise disappeared. The people went away. But from the tortoise they received the proverb: "Stupidity doesn't kill a man, but it makes him sweat."

The Cat, the Dog, and Death

In ancient times, in the beginning of things, God had not yet made up his mind about whether the creatures he had created should live forever. The question had not yet been decided.

The cat and the dog had a discussion about the matter.

The cat said, "It is my opinion that when creatures have lived their lives, they should not go on living forever."

The dog said, "Oh, no, on the contrary—I think that we should live for all time."

"No," the cat insisted, "No one should live forever. When he has lived his life, that is enough."

The dog said, "I will go to see God about this matter. I shall insist that all creatures should live forever."

The cat declared, "I too will go to see God about this question."

They parted. The dog considered how he could delay the cat. He took some butter, placed it on a banana leaf, and set it by the edge of the trail where the cat would not miss seeing it.

As for the cat, he too considered how he might delay the dog. He found a large bone and placed it near the trail where the dog would not fail to see it. He went home, bathed himself, and dressed. Then he began the journey to God's house.

The dog also bathed and dressed and set out for God's house.

When the cat came to the place where the butter was waiting for him, he ignored it and continued on his way.

When the dog came to the place where the bone was waiting for him, he smelled it. He said to himself, "This is no time to stop." But as he passed the bone, his head turned so that his nose was pointing directly at it. He stopped and sat down. He said to his nose, "This is no time for pointing." He started out again, but his head turned further and further, until his nose was pointing backward toward his tail. At last the dog went back and began to gnaw on the bone.

The cat arrived at God's house. God asked him, "What is it you have come to tell me?"

The cat replied, "I have come to say that when a person has lived out his life, then he should live no longer."

God thought about the matter. At last he said, "Very well, so it shall be."

When the dog had finished gnawing on the bone, he continued on his way to God's house. God asked him, "What is it you have come to tell me?"

The dog answered, "I have come to say that all creatures should live forever."

But God said, "It is too late. The decision has been made."

So it is that no creature lives forever. Because the dog could not resist the bone lying by the trail, he did not arrive in time. With the dog it is still this way. He cannot pass a bone anywhere without giving it a great deal of attention.

Sweet Misery

A WOMAN was going to market one day, with a large calabash of syrup on her head. As she walked along the road, she tripped, and the calabash fell to the ground and broke. When she saw the broken calabash, with the syrup running out, she cried, "Oh, misery! Oh, misery!"

A dog who was nearby heard her cry out, "Oh, misery!" He wondered, "What is this misery the woman is talking about?" And he came to investigate. He found the broken calabash of syrup lying in the road. He smelled it and tasted it. It was delicious, and he began to lick it up, saying, "Oh, this misery is very sweet! Misery is very wonderful!"

When he had licked it all up, he went away. He met a cat to whom he said, "Oh, I have had wonderful luck! A woman spilled a calabash of misery and left it behind. It was so sweet! It was so delicious!"

The cat was envious. He wanted some of what the dog had discovered. He went to God to ask for some.

God said, "What is it you want from me?"

The cat said, "Misery."

God said the cat could have it. He went in the back room and found a sack. He put something in the sack. He gave the sack to the cat, saying, "Here is your misery. Open it when you get home, not before."

The cat took the bag and went home. When he arrived, he opened the bag quickly. A dog jumped out and began to chase him. The dog has never stopped chasing the cat. Thus it was that the cat got his misery. It is still with him.

The Gun, the Pot, and the Hat

ONE day Madame Malice said to Ti Malice, "Tonight my relatives are coming to visit. We have only three chickens. You had better get something to feed them."

"Well," Ti Malice said, "I will go hunting. Prepare the chickens while I am gone."

He took his old gun and headed for the woods. After a while he became tired, and he sat down under a tree to think things over.

Ti Malice was just beginning to make some headway with his thinking when he heard a noise like a drove of wild pigs crashing through the underbrush. And then, *ba-o!* A stone hit the tree right over his head. Ti Malice jumped to his feet and cocked his gun. There was a grunting and scuffling, and Uncle Bouki charged into the clearing. In his hand he had a slingshot made of a bamboo tube and a piece of rubber.

"Where did that guinea hen go?" Bouki said.

"Guinea hen?" Ti Malice said. "You think you could hit a guinea hen with *that?*"

"Yes," Bouki said, "that is why I am doing it."

"Too bad you don't have something like this," Ti Malice said, holding up his rusty gun.

"Pardon me for laughing," Bouki said. "Is that supposed to be a gun?

"You're just like other ignorant people," Ti Malice said. "This isn't just a gun. It's Kokoto."

"Kokoto? It looks like something left over from the Revolution."

"My friend," Ti Malice said, "you are only showing your stupidity. Kokoto isn't something to laugh at. Look at this!" He pointed the gun straight up in the air and—*peaou-u!*—fired it without aiming.

"What do you think you're shooting?" Bouki said.

"A bird," Malice replied.

"Where?" Bouki said. "I didn't see any bird."

"It's too far away to see," Ti Malice said. "Kokoto sees it for me."

"Wah! Listen to that!" Bouki said. "Where's the bird now?"

"When I shoot birds with this gun," Ti Malice said, "I don't even have to pick them up. They fall right in my yard."

"Wah! Wah! Listen to that!" Bouki shouted. "I can't stand it!"

"Look," Ti Malice said, and he pointed his gun in the air and fired again.

"I didn't see anything," Bouki said. "What were you firing at that time?"

"Another bird," Ti Malice said. "That makes two."

"And where is this bird falling?" Bouki asked.

"In my yard," Ti Malice said. "My wife will pick it up and cook it."

"Wah! I can't stand it!" Bouki said, holding his sides. Ti Malice pointed the gun at the clouds and fired again.

"I suppose that makes three birds?" Bouki said.

"Yes, that's enough for today," Ti Malice said. "Now I'll go home."

"I'll go with you," Bouki said. "I want to see for myself."

They walked back to Ti Malice's house together. As they came into the yard, Bouki saw Madame Malice there, and his mouth fell open, for there she was, picking the last feathers off three fat birds.

"Oh-oh!" Bouki said.

"What do you say now?" Ti Malice asked.

Bouki didn't make a sound for a moment. He was busy thinking. Then he said, "Friend Malice, I've got to have Kokoto! I'll buy it!"

"Buy it? Oh, no," Ti Malice said. "Kokoto is one thing I don't care to sell. Not Kokoto."

"Look!" Bouki said, pulling some money from his pocket. "I'll give you twenty-five gourdes!"

"Don't joke, friend Bouki," Ti Malice said solemnly. "Kokoto isn't for sale."

"Thirty!" Bouki said.

Ti Malice shook his head. "No, I'd just as soon sell my wife or children as Kokoto."

"Fifty gourdes and forty centimes!" Bouki said. "It's all I have! I was saving it to buy a burro!"

"Are you sure it's all you have?" Ti Malice said.

Bouki turned his empty pocket inside out.

"All right, then," Ti Malice said. "I'm doing it only because you want it so much." He gave the gun to Bouki and took the money. "However, there's one thing you have to know about this gun. Don't let anyone else touch it or it won't work for you."

The next morning Bouki got up at daybreak to go hunting. He said to Madame Bouki: "Now, keep your eyes open! Every once in a while–*blippe!*–a guinea hen will fall in the yard! Every time I shoot–*blippe!*–there's another bird! All you have to do is pick them up and fix them for dinner."

"What are you talking about?" Madame Bouki said.

"Never mind," Bouki said. "Just watch the guinea hens come all morning–*blippe! blippe! blippe!*" And he went out to hunt, with Kokoto on his shoulder.

After a while Bouki loaded the gun and pointed it in the air–*peaou-u!*

"That's one," he said, and loaded the gun again.

He pointed and fired again. *Peaou-u!*

"That's two."

He reloaded and fired again. *Peaou-u!*

"Three."

Peaou-u!

"Four."

He lay on his back and kept loading and firing. *Peaou-u! Peaou-u! Peaou-u!*

After a while he fell asleep in the warm sun. When he woke up, he loaded and fired again. *Peaou-u! Peaou-u! Peaou-u!* At last he said, "That makes twenty-one." He tried to imagine Madame Bouki's surprise as the guinea hens dropped *blippe, blippe, blippe* into the yard. He started for home, running.

When he came to his gate, he saw Madame Bouki working over something. He hurried across the yard. Madame Bouki was washing clothes.

"Where are the guinea hens?" Bouki asked.

"Guinea hens? What guinea hens?" Madame Bouki asked.

"The ones I shot with Kokoto," Bouki said.

Madame Bouki looked sadly at Bouki and shook her head.

"Lightning strike him!" Bouki shouted. He started at a run for Ti Malice's place.

Now, just as Bouki was coming up the path, Ti Malice took a big iron pot of cornmeal off the fire and set it in the middle of the yard to cool. The pot was so hot that the cornmeal kept bubbling and boiling.

"Give me back my fifty gourdes and forty centimes!" Bouki shouted.

"Quiet," Ti Malice said. "I'm just finishing up this special pot of cornmeal."

"Never mind your cornmeal!" Bouki said. "Kokoto is nothing but a rusted old pipe!"

"Shhhh!" Ti Malice said. "You see that cornmeal boiling?"

"Certainly it's boiling," Bouki said. "What of it?"

"But, as you can see, there's no fire under it," Ti Malice said.

"That's true," Bouki said, scratching his head.

"Did you ever before see a pot that could cook without fire?"

"Wah!" Bouki said. "How do you do it?"

"It's my pot that does it," Ti Malice said.

"Oh-oh! That's a pot worth owning!" Bouki said. "This

Kokoto isn't any good at all, but I'd certainly like to have that pot!"

"You probably let someone handle Kokoto. I told you not to let anyone touch it," Ti Malice said. "That's what spoiled it."

"Here," Bouki said, "take the gun back and let me have the pot instead."

"What? Let you have Dokodo? Oh, I couldn't let you have Dokodo. It's the only pot of its kind anywhere."

"Look," Bouki said. "I'll give you back Kokoto and ten gourdes more!"

"Oh, no, not Dokodo," Ti Malice said.

"Fifteen gourdes!" Bouki said. "I've been saving it for a new roof for my house."

"All right," Ti Malice said at last, "but only because you're my old friend."

Bouki picked up the hot iron pot and started home.

"Don't let anyone touch it," Ti Malice called after him.

"Ouch!" Bouki answered as the hot cornmeal splashed on his feet.

When he got home, he waved the pot in the air. "Malice definitely made a mistake when he tried to do business with me," he told Madame Bouki. "I made him take his gun back."

"What's that thing you are waving around?" Madame Bouki asked.

"Don't show your ignorance," Bouki said. "This is Dokodo."

"Why don't you just stay home and grow potatoes?" Madame Bouki said.

In the morning, before going out to the field to work,

Bouki set Dokodo by the door on three stones. He put bananas, plantains, and a yam into it. Then he put in beans until the pot was full to the top.

"What are you doing now?" Madame Bouki asked.

"Never mind that," Bouki said. "Just see that you don't touch Dokodo, you hear? By tonight it will be all cooked."

He took his hoe and went to his cornfield. All day he kept thinking about the delicious food that would be waiting for him when he returned. "What a friend Ti Malice is!" he kept saying over and over.

When his work was done, Bouki hurried home. There was no one in the yard. He ran to where the pot sat by the door. He looked closely. He poked at the food with a stick. The bananas and beans and plantains were as raw and hard as they could be.

"Wah!" he shouted. "That Ti Malice has done it again!"

He grabbed the pot and ran to Ti Malice's house. But there was no one home. So he headed for the market. Inside the market he raced around like a bull, stepping on people's rice and potatoes and knocking over piles of baskets and clay pots. He found Madame Malice selling tobacco leaves.

"Where's that no good Ti Malice?" he shouted. "I'll salt him down like a dried fish!"

"He's at the Ti Bobine Cafe," Madame Malice said.

Bouki raced out of the market to the Ti Bobine Cafe. He peeked through the window, and there, sure enough, was Ti Malice sitting at a table eating a big plate of rice and beans. Bouki stood waiting for Ti Malice to come out. The smells from inside made him hungry, and he kept peeking at the rice and beans Ti Malice was eating.

TI BOBINE CA

What Bouki didn't know was that whenever Ti Malice came to market, he always saved a few melons to trade for his dinner at the Ti Bobine Cafe. He would turn in the melons when he arrived, then order his food. So Bouki was amazed when he saw Ti Malice get up, put on his hat, say good-by, and walk out.

Bouki reached out and caught hold of Ti Malice by the arm as he came through the door.

"Aha!" he said. "So this old pot will cook without fire, will it?"

"Oh-oh!" Ti Malice said. "Uncle Bouki!"

"You've robbed me!" Bouki shouted. "Fifty gourdes and forty centimes for Kokoto, and fifteen gourdes more for Dokodo! I'll take you to court!"

"Madame Bouki must have touched Dokodo," Ti Malice said. "I told you to be careful!"

"She did?" Bouki said. "Oh, wait till I get my hands on her!"

"Well, I have to go now," Ti Malice said.

"Just a minute," Bouki said. "How did you manage to get out of the cafe without paying?"

"Oh, that's Popo," Ti Malice said.

"What's Popo?" Bouki asked.

"The hat. It's the only one of its kind. If you wear it, you don't have to pay. You put it on your head and say good-by and go home."

"Look," Bouki said. "We can straighten everything out. I'll give you back Dokodo for Popo."

"Popo? This old hat? Oh, no, nobody would want to be seen wearing it."

"I'd like to get something to eat," Bouki said. "I'll give you Dokodo and fifty centimes for Popo."

"Well," Ti Malice said, "I don't know . . ."

"Don't forget that you are my child's godfather," Bouki said. "I'll give you the pot and five gourdes for Popo!"

"Hmmm . . ." Ti Malice said.

"Ten gourdes!" Bouki said. "It's absolutely all I have!"

"Very well, then," Ti Malice said. "Just because you're an old friend." He gave the hat to Bouki and took the pot and the ten gourdes. "Remember, all you do is to put the hat on your head and say good-by."

Bouki went into the Ti Bobine Cafe. He sat down and ordered chicken and rice and beans. Then he ordered yucca cakes and, after that, cornmeal pudding. He ate a great deal. He ordered a glass of wine. When he was finished with that, he ordered four cigars.

"For once in my life I've had enough to eat," Bouki said.

He got up and nodded his head to the proprietor. He put his hat on his head.

"Good-by," he said.

"Good-by," the proprietor said. "But didn't you forget something?"

"No," Bouki said. "I said good-by."

"You said good-by?"

"I said good-by," Bouki said. He headed for the door.

"It's nice of you to say good-by," the proprietor said. "But how about the bill?"

"You must be blind," Bouki said. "I have Popo on my head."

"You have *what* on your head?"

"You must be deaf too," Bouki said. "I have *Popo* on my head."

He went out the door. The proprietor shouted for

the police. Bouki began to run. The police ran after him. They raced down the main street, then through the market. When he came to the edge of town, Bouki headed for the hills.

He passed his friend Tonton Cabrite on the trail.

"What's wrong?" Tonton Cabrite asked.

"Ti Malice did it again! I have Popo on my head!" Bouki shouted as he went by.

The Lizard's Big Dance

ZANDOLITE, the tree lizard, went one time to the Vodoun priest to find out why his crops were not growing properly. He said, "*Bocor*, my yams and my potatoes dry up in the ground. What is the matter?"

The Vodoun priest took out his divining shells, threw them on the ground several times, and studied them. Then he said, "Zandolite, the shells say that you are being punished because you have forgotten to give a service for your ancestors. They are angry. If you want your crops to grow, you will have to give a big festival for them."

Zandolite went home. He told his wife. He sent his children to tell his brothers and sisters who lived in different villages. And he prepared a big service for the ancestors. He announced to people everywhere that he was giving a feast and dance at such and such a time. To provide music for the dance, he arranged to have the finest drummers he could find.

The time for the festival came. It was to last three days and nights. People arrived in their best clothes. There was a great crowd. The drummers began to play, and people began to dance. All night long there was drumming, and the sound went out around the countryside. While some people danced, others ate. The drums did not stop. When the sun came up, people were still dancing. The festival went on and on.

The noise was deafening. God heard it. It kept him from sleeping at night, and when day came, he couldn't concentrate on his work. Finally he thought he would have to put a stop to it. So he called St. John and instructed him to go down and order the lizard to bring his service to an end.

St. John went down and walked along the trail to Zandolite's house. There was a great stream of people coming and going, and the din rang in St. John's ears. When he came to Zandolite's gate, the lizard was there to greet him. "I bring you a message," St. John said.

But Zandolite replied, "Eat first, drink first, then we shall talk."

The lizard brought him in to the very center of things and sat him down as a guest of honor near the drummers. He brought St. John food, and he brought him kola to drink. The drums went on and on: *katap-katap-katap-katap*. And before long St. John was moving his feet, and the next thing he knew he was dancing with the other guests.

Quite a long time went by, and when St. John didn't come back, God thought, "I wonder what's the matter? I sent St. John down a long time ago, and the noise is still going on." He called St. Patrick and said, "Go down and find St. John and put an end to that noise at the lizard's house."

So St. Patrick went down too, and when he came to Zandolite's house, the lizard met him at the gate and brought him in. "I have a message," St. Patrick said.

But Zandolite replied, "Eat and drink first, then we shall talk."

He sat St. Patrick down by the drums and brought him food and kola. Before he was finished eating and drinking, St. Patrick's feet were moving, and in no time at all he was dancing with the crowd.

God waited quite a while. Then he called St. Peter. He said, "The noise down there is too much. I can't sleep at night. I can't do my work in the daytime. I sent St. John down to take care of it. He didn't come back. I sent St. Patrick down to take care of it. He didn't come back. Go down and find them. Tell them to get back here as fast as they can. And you, before you come back, tell all those people and the drummers to go away. I need a little peace and quiet."

St. Peter went down. He felt very sad that St. John and St. Patrick hadn't done what God told them to do. When he arrived at Zandolite's place, the crowd was bigger than ever, the singing was loud, and the drums were echoing from one hill to another. Zandolite met him at the gate. St. Peter was stern. He said, "I am sent with a message."

The lizard said, "Yes, yes, but first come in and join the service for the ancestors. Eat, drink, and then we shall talk."

He took St. Peter in and sat him down near the drummers. He brought him food and kola. St. Peter ate. He drank. His feet began to move. He began to dance. And then, like St. John and St. Patrick, St. Peter became lost in the crowd.

Hours went by. The noise was not less but more. And

when after a long time St. Peter didn't return, God said, "I will go down myself. I will put an end to this affair once and for all."

He went down. As he neared the lizard's house, he had to push through crowds of people to get to the gate. Zandolite met him. God said, "Zandolite, you give me great trouble. I sent St. John first, then St. Patrick, then St. Peter. You did not listen. And now I am angry."

"Come in, come in," Zandolite cried. "Eat first, drink first, then we shall talk."

"I shall not eat and drink first," said God. "I shall not eat and drink at all."

"This is a feast for the family ancestors," Zandolite said. "Don't you wish to pay them respect?"

So God changed his mind, and Zandolite brought him to a chair near the drummers and gave him food and kola.

God frowned at the noise. It was much worse here than at home. He ate. He drank. First one foot moved a little. Then the other moved a little. Then the first foot twitched. Then the second foot twitched. And before he had finished his kola, God found himself dancing with the others.

The drums went on and on. At midnight of the third day the festival came to an end. People began to go home. Zandolite was so tired that he fell asleep on a bench. The people had eaten two cows, four goats, one pig, and eighteen chickens.

God looked around at the remains of the celebration. He beckoned to St. John, St. Patrick, and St. Peter, and they went away quietly so as not to wake up Zandolite.

As for the lizard's crops, they stopped drying up in the ground. Instead, they grew bountifully. And why should they not grow, since St. John, St. Patrick, St. Peter, and God himself had come to dance in his house?

Bouki Buys a Burro

IT WAS planting time, and Bouki went out to his garden to plant yams. First he had to chop down all the weeds and brush and burn them. Then he had to hoe up the earth to make it soft. While Bouki was working like this, his boy Tijean came by with a calabash of water on his head.

"What are you planting here, Papa?" Tijean asked.

"Tijean," Bouki said, "this is going to be the finest garden around here. And before you can turn around, I'll have the biggest and fattest burro they ever saw in these mountains."

"You are going to plant a burro?" Tijean asked.

"Listen to him!" Bouki said. "Who ever heard of planting burros?" He put down his hoe and lighted his pipe. "Look," he said, "I am making a garden now. Anybody can see that. When I have finished hoeing up the ground, I'll plant yams. After a while the yams are grown. Then I dig one yam up, just one. I take it to the market in the city to sell it. It's the biggest yam that ever came out of the mountains. People say, 'Look at that yam, will you! Bouki grew it!' They crowd and push to get a look at it. They are making a tremendous noise. Everything gets kicked upside down. People are stepping on each other's toes. They are trampling on a pile of beans. They knock down the clay cooking pots. There is so much noise the police come to restore order. When the police see my yam, they are amazed. Everyone wants to buy it. But you know who gets it? The President's wife. She carries on. She says she has to have that yam no matter what. It is for the President's dinner. She pays a tremendous price, one hundred gourdes. Then after that, I take the money and buy a fat, strong burro, almost as big as a mule."

"Wye!" Tijean shouted. "We have a burro!"

"Just a minute," Bouki said. "You mean *I* have a burro." He puffed on his pipe. "Whenever I go to market now with yams and potatoes, Marie—that's her name—does all the work."

"Wye! Marie does all the work!" Tijean shouted. He picked up a long stick, straddled it, and began running in a big circle around the garden. "Allé! Allé!" Tijean shouted. He began to whip her to make her go faster.

Bouki watched Tijean. He frowned. He called to Tijean to stop, but Tijean was jumping and running in wild zigzags around the clearing. Bouki began to run too, chasing Tijean over the lumpy ground. He caught Tijean by the collar and shook him.

"So!" he said. "So! Is this the kind of fellow you are? Without even asking? You ride my burro without even saying please? I'll show you! Get off! Get off at once!"

Bouki and Tijean were making so much noise that all the neighbors came out to see what was happening. They stood in the garden watching Bouki and Tijean wrestling and tugging at the stick.

"Get off her and stay off!" Bouki shouted.

"Bouki, what's the matter?" someone called.

"It's a family affair!" Bouki answered. "He rides my burro without even a please!"

"What burro?" someone else asked. "You don't have any burro."

Bouki let go of Tijean and began to look thoughtful.

"It's the burro he bought for the yam," Tijean said. "He won't let me ride her."

"What yam?" someone said.

"There," Bouki said, pointing at his hoe lying on the ground. "I'm growing it."

"But you didn't even plant it yet," someone said.

"The President's wife bought it," Tijean said.

"You haven't even finished hoeing the ground," someone said.

"Just the same, Marie's too expensive to be ridden like that," Bouki said.

"It's not a real burro," Tijean said.

Bouki said, "You admit that you didn't ask my permission, don't you?"

"Yes," Tijean answered.

The neighbors shook their heads and went home.

"I'll tell you one thing," Bouki said to Tijean. "You could have at least said please."

Ticoumba and the President

THERE was a man named Ticoumba. He was walking in the street one day when the President came riding along in his carriage. All the men in the street took off their hats as a sign of respect, but Ticoumba didn't take off his hat. The President stopped his carriage. He said to Ticoumba, "You don't respect me. When the President rides by, everyone takes off his hat."

Ticoumba answered, "Where I come from, we take off our hats only when the hearse goes by."

The President was annoyed. He said, "You are insolent. I am warning you. *I never want to see your face again!*" And he rode on.

Another day when Ticoumba saw the President's carriage approaching, he looked around and saw a big limekiln. He quickly stuck his head into the opening of the limekiln and remained that way. When the President looked at the limekiln, he saw the back side of Ticoumba greeting him. He stopped his carriage and shouted, "Who is it that salutes me this way with the wrong end?"

Ticoumba replied, his voice muffled inside the limekiln, "It is I, Ticoumba."

"Come out at once!" the President ordered. And when Ticoumba took his head out and turned around, the President said, "Ah, didn't I have a word with you the other day?"

"Yes," Ticoumba answered. "I did what you told me. You said, '*I never want to see your face again.*' Therefore, I put my head in the limekiln so that you wouldn't see it."

The President said: "Man, you are a troublemaker. I warn you again, there is no room for you here. I never want to see you again—*clothed or unclothed, dressed or naked*. Do you understand?"

"Yes, my President, I understand," Ticoumba answered. He went away.

But it happened one day that Ticoumba was near the seashore when the President's carriage came along. He took off his clothes and draped a fishnet over his head, and he stood there waiting. A laughing crowd gathered around Ticoumba. When the President's carriage drew up, the President went into the crowd to see what the attraction was. There he saw Ticoumba with no clothes but with a fishnet hanging over him.

"Ticoumba! We meet once more!" the President said sternly. "So you have violated my orders!"

"No, my President, I did just what you told me," Ticoumba replied. "You said you never wanted to see me again *clothed or unclothed, dressed or naked.* I am not dressed because my clothes are here beside me on the ground. And I am not naked because, as you can see, I am covered with this fishnet."

The President said: "You are clever, but you are a

rascal. You twist my words around, though you understand my meaning very well. This time you can't twist my words. Listen carefully: *If I ever again catch you walking on Haitian ground, I will have you shot!* Do you understand?"

Ticoumba said, "Yes, my President, I understand."

He picked up his clothes and went away. He thought about his problem. Then he boarded a sailing boat and went to Barbados. When the President heard that Ticoumba was gone, he was pleased.

But one day when the President was near the waterfront, he saw a sailing boat dock there. And off the boat came Ticoumba. The President ordered the police to arrest him. They brought him to the President's house. A large crowd gathered to witness the affair.

The President said, "Ticoumba, say your prayers. You have refused to obey my orders. Do you remember what I told you?"

"Yes, my President," Ticoumba answered. "You said that if you ever again caught me *walking on Haitian ground*, you would have me shot."

"Very well. I have caught you," the President said. And to the police he said, "Take Ticoumba away and shoot him!"

"Just one moment, my President," Ticoumba said. "I did what you told me to."

"How is that?" the President asked.

"Why, I took a boat to Barbados," Ticoumba said, "and in Bridgetown I bought a large pair of boots. I filled the bottom of the boots with sand, and then I put them on. As everyone knows, Barbados belongs to England. So you see, my President, wherever I go, I am *walking on British soil.*"

The people looked at Ticoumba's boots. They laughed. The President laughed too. He said, "Ticoumba, you are the first man that ever outtalked me. Let us say the matter is finished. But there is just one thing—don't let me ever catch you without your boots on!"

And since that time, Ticoumba has worn his boots everywhere.

Nananbouclou and the Piece of Fire

IN ANCIENT times only the deities lived in the world. There were Shango, the god of lightning; Ogoun, the god of ironsmiths; Agwé, the god of the sea; Legba, the messenger god; and others. Their mother was Nananbouclou; she was the first of all the gods.

One day Legba came to the city and said: "A strange thing has happened. A great piece of fire has fallen from the sky." The gods went out with Legba, and he showed them where the piece of fire lay, scorching the land on all sides. Because Agwé was god of the sea, he brought the ocean in to surround the piece of fire and prevent it from burning up the world. Then they approached the fire and began to discuss how they could take it back to the city. Because Ogoun was the god of ironsmiths, he forged a chain around the great piece of fire and captured it. But there remained the problem of how to transport it. So Shango, the god of lightning, fastened it to a thunderbolt and hurled it to the city. Then they returned.

Nananbouclou, the mother of the gods, admired what

they had found. And she said, "This is indeed a great thing." But the gods began to quarrel over who should have it.

Legba, the messenger god, said: "It was I who discovered it. Therefore, it belongs to me."

Agwé, the god of the sea, said: "I brought the ocean to surround it and keep it from eating up the earth. Therefore, it should be mine."

Ogoun, the ironworker, said: "Did I not forge a chain to wrap around the fire and capture it? Therefore, I am the proper owner."

And Shango, the god of lightning, said: "Who brought the piece of fire home? It was I who transported it on a thunderbolt. Therefore, there is no doubt whatsoever, it is mine."

They argued this way back and forth. They became angry with one another.

At last Nananbouclou halted the argument. She said: "This thing that has been brought back is beautiful. But before it came, there was harmony, and now there are bad words. This person claims it, that person claims it. Therefore, shall we continue to live with it in our midst?"

Nananbouclou took hold of the piece of fire and hurled it high into the sky.

There it has remained ever since. It is known by the name of Baiacou. It is the evening star.

The Fishermen

TI MALICE and Bouki decided one time that they would be partners and go fishing together. People said to Bouki, "Why do you go into business with Ti Malice? He is clever. The affair will end badly."

But Bouki answered, "A man does not get rich if he selects a fool for a partner."

Bouki and Ti Malice put their money together and bought a boat. Ti Malice took some paint and painted the name *St. Pierre* on the bow of the boat. Then he sprinkled rum over it and said, "I christen you *St. Pierre*."

"Just a minute," Bouki said. "What do you think you are doing?"

"I merely christened the boat," Ti Malice said.

"Don't you think I have something to say about the matter?" Bouki said. "Give me the paint!"

Bouki painted the name *St. Jacques* on the stern of the boat. Then he sprinkled rum over it and said, "I christen the back end *St. Jacques!*"

Ti Malice ran the sail up and down three times to see if it was all right. "Just a minute," Bouki said. He ran the sail up and down five times to see if it was all right.

They took the boat to sea and put their net in the water. When it came time to haul it in, Ti Malice said: "Just rest, Bouki. Since I am the boss, I will do the hauling."

"Just a minute," Bouki said. "Nobody made you the boss. I will do the hauling."

So Bouki tugged and hauled all by himself until the net was in. Again they put the net in the water, and Ti Malice said: "Rest now. Since I am the big man around here, I will do the hauling."

"Oh, no," Bouki said. "Nobody appointed you to be the big man in this crew. I will do the hauling myself."

Again Bouki wrestled and tugged at the net until it was in. All day it was this way. At last they sailed for home with their catch in the bottom of the boat. The wind began to drop, and the boat sailed more slowly.

"Go, *St. Pierre!*" Ti Malice said from where he sat in the front.

"Go, *St. Jacques!*" Bouki said from the back where he sat at the tiller.

Ti Malice sang a song to Loko, the god of wind:

"Wind, wind, wind, Loko,
Malice asks for wind, oh!
Wind, wind, wind, Loko,
Malice asks for wind!"

"Just a minute," Bouki said, "I didn't hear my name mentioned." And he sang:

"Wind, wind, wind, Loko,
Bouki asks for wind, oh!
Wind, wind, wind, Loko,
Bouki asks for wind!"

The wind died. The boat stopped moving.

"Since I am the strongest, I will row," Ti Malice said.

"Just a minute," Bouki said. "No one appointed you the strongest. I will do the rowing."

So Bouki rowed and Ti Malice steered.

They came ashore and took the fish from the bottom of the boat.

"They look small today," Ti Malice said. "How shall we divide?"

"You take one, I'll take one, until they're all gone," Bouki said.

"No, they're too small," Ti Malice said. "Tomorrow they'll probably be bigger. You take them all today, and I'll take them all tomorrow."

"Just a minute," Bouki said. "Don't tell me what to do! *You* take them all today, and *I'll* take them all tomorrow."

So Ti Malice gathered the fish and took them home. The next day they went out again. When they fished, Ti Malice said he would haul because he was the boss, but Bouki wouldn't permit him to be boss and hauled the net in alone. When they had to row with the oars, Bouki refused to admit that Ti Malice was strongest, and he rowed the boat himself. When they came to shore, Ti Malice said that Bouki should have the catch because the fish were so small, but Bouki protested: "Oh, no, my friend, do not try to outsmart me. You take the catch today, and I'll take the catch tomorrow."

Every day Bouki rowed and hauled. Every day Ti Malice took the fish home. Time passed. Bouki worked harder and harder and got thinner and thinner. Ti Malice argued and rested and got fatter and fatter.

Once the fish net got torn, and Ti Malice said, "Since

I have the most responsibility around here, I will take the net home for Madame Malice to mend."

"Oh no you won't!" Bouki said. "Who do you think you are? I will take the net home myself for Madame Bouki to mend!"

Then one afternoon when they were coming in with the catch, Bouki began to think. He was very hungry. He looked at Malice and saw how fat he was. He thought some more and started counting on his fingers. When they reached the shore, Ti Malice said: "They are so small, you probably want me to take them again."

But before Ti Malice could get the fish strung on a stick, Bouki took his machete out of his belt and said: "Can you possibly explain why you are so fat and I am so hungry?"

Ti Malice turned and ran. Bouki ran after him. They raced through the marketplace, and Ti Malice tried to get lost in the crowd. He made a sound like a chicken, duk-a-duk-a-duk, but Bouki kept coming after him. Ti Malice ran into a church by the front door and out by the back, joining in the singing as he went through. Bouki was still coming. When Ti Malice saw a hole in a wall, he tried to climb through. But he had eaten too much fish, and he stuck at the hips, his head on one side of the wall and his legs on the other.

When Bouki came to the wall, he looked up and down the street. All he saw was Ti Malice's back end protruding from the wall. He tipped his hat politely and said, "Excuse me, have you seen Ti Malice?"

"Push me, and I'll tell you," Ti Malice answered.

So Bouki pushed, and Ti Malice went through the wall and was gone.

Bouki returned to the shore where the boat rested on the sand.

"I declare the partnership dissolved," he said.

And he sawed the boat in half and moored the part named *St. Jacques* securely on the beach.

Who Is the Older?

A GOAT and a bull met one time in the field. The bull ignored the goat. But the goat stood before him and said, "I'm an older man than you."

The bull looked at the goat with amazement. He said, "No, I am older than you."

The goat said, "Son, run home to your father."

The bull said, "Does your mother know you are out here alone?"

The goat said, "Your big sister ought to be taking care of you."

The bull said, "Why are you always saying *baa, baa?* Are you calling for your grandmother?"

The goat said, "Don't talk to your elders that way. Don't you see I have a beard?"

The bull replied, "Good Lord! What is the country coming to? The little ones have beards, but I, who am big, big, big, have no beard!" Tears came to his eyes.

"One side," the goat said, "and let an elderly gentleman pass."

The Voyage Below the Water

There was a country man named Bordeau. He had worked hard all his life, and he became wealthy. He had many children. He was happy. Then, one day, his wife died.

There were the ceremonies. He had a mahogany coffin made. She was buried.

Bordeau hardly said a word. He sat in his house silently. If the children spoke, he did not seem to hear. The sons went out to take care of the fields, but Bordeau did not go with them. His old friends came to pass an hour or two with him in the evening, but he said nothing. When food was brought to him, he refused to eat. He didn't seem to know whether it was day or night.

The time went by. The evening arrived for the saying of last prayers for the dead woman. Relatives and friends came from the villages, the Vodoun priest came, the drummers came. And as they were preparing for the customary praying, dancing, and singing in the courtyard, Bordeau came out of the house and asked them all to go home.

"Bordeau," one of his old friends said, "this is the night for last prayers. Do not send the people home. Let us hold the service."

Bordeau answered: "For the praying, the singing, the dancing, and the feast, I care nothing. What does all this mean to me now that my wife is gone? Go away. I cannot bear the sound of music. I will not dance, I will not eat. My grief is too great."

"Bordeau," one of his friends said, "death comes to every family. It spares no one. Today it is there. Tomorrow it is here."

Another one said, "Bordeau, the dead cannot return. Do not treat yourself this way. Let the last prayers be said. Let the people dance. And let the feast be held."

"No," Bordeau said. "My house shall remain silent."

"Bordeau," the Vodoun priest said, "your wife now lives

beneath the water with the ancestors. We do not give ourselves to silence and grief forever because one we love has gone there."

But Bordeau would not be persuaded.

So the Vodoun priest said: "Bordeau, I will go beneath the water to find your wife. I will try to speak with her."

"Very well," Bordeau said. "But if you do not bring her back, then I will not speak again, I will not eat, my land can grow back to wild grass, and my house can rot and fall where it stands."

The Vodoun priest made preparations. He took his sacred beaded rattle in his hand and went down to the edge of the river. The people brought animals to sacrifice. There was a ceremony. They sang. And at midnight the Vodoun priest walked slowly into the river, deeper and deeper, until he disappeared.

The people waited on the bank of the river for three days, and at midnight of the third day, the Vodoun priest came out of the river, shaking his sacred rattle. There was great excitement. The people took him to Bordeau's house. They entered. Bordeau was sitting there.

"He has returned!" the people shouted to Bordeau. "Our Vodoun priest has gone below the water and come back!"

"Where is my wife?" Bordeau said.

"Listen, Bordeau," the Vodoun priest said. "I went below the water. I went far. There was a long road. I followed it. There were hills, and I crossed them. There was a forest, and I passed through it. I came to the City of the Ancestors. There were many, many people there. My father was among them. My mother was among them. Your father and mother were there. Your grandfathers were there. Everyone who was ever here before us was there. I searched for your wife. I went everywhere. I came to the marketplace, and there I found her selling beans. I said, 'Your husband Bordeau is grieving. He does not eat, he does not sleep, he does not speak. He says, "If my wife does not return from the dead, may my house fall in upon me." I have come to bring you back.' Your wife said this, Bordeau. She said, 'It is pleasant to have someone grieve for you. But I live here now, below the water. When one dies, he does not return. Tell Bordeau to bring the grief to an end. Tell him to eat. For when one is dead, he is dead, but when one is alive, he must live.' Bordeau, your wife gave me one of the gold earrings she wore. She said it was for you."

The Vodoun priest took his kerchief from his pocket, and from the kerchief he took an earring, which he gave to Bordeau.

Bordeau looked at the earring, saying, "Yes, this is my wife's earring."

He sat silently then for a long while, looking at the earring. At last he said:

"My wife has sent me a message from below the water. She said, 'When one is alive, he must live.' So it shall be. Let us hold the service of the last prayers. Let the food be prepared. Let the drummers drum. I will eat. I will dance."

Bouki Cuts Wood

Bouki went out to cut wood in the Pine Forest. He climbed a tree, sat on a branch, and began to chop with his machete. A traveler came along and stopped to watch him. "Wye!" the man said. "Just look at that! He's sitting on the same branch that he's cutting. In a few minutes the branch will fall, and he'll be on the ground. How foolish can a person be?"

Bouki stopped chopping. "Who is the stupid man that calls me foolish?" he called down. "Are you trying to foretell the future? Only God knows what is going to happen."

The traveler said no more. He went on his way.

Bouki resumed his chopping. Just as the man predicted, the branch broke, and Bouki came down with it.

Bouki gave it some thought. "It was just as the man predicted," Bouki said. "He must be a *bocor*, a diviner."

He jumped on his donkey and rode after the man. When he caught up with him on the trail, he said, "*Bocor*, you told the truth. I didn't know you were a diviner. You predicted the future, and it came out just as you said. So tell me one more thing: When am I going to die?"

The traveler answered, "Who in his right mind wants to know that? But if you insist, I'll tell you." He thought for a moment. "You'll die when your donkey brays three times," he said, and continued on his way.

"Thank you, *bocor*, thank you!" Bouki called after him. Then he said to himself, "Three times! This donkey is braying all the time!"

And as soon as they started back, the donkey opened his mouth and brayed.

"Stop! That's one already!" Bouki shouted.

The donkey brayed again.

"Stop! Stop! That's twice already!" Bouki shouted.

And as the donkey opened its mouth and stretched its neck to bray again, Bouki leaned over the animal's head and tried to push its jaws together. He struggled. The donkey struggled. Then it came—another bray.

"That's the end," Bouki said. "He brayed three times! Therefore, I must be dead!"

So he fell off the donkey and lay motionless at the side of the trail. He didn't try to get up because dead men lie where they fall.

After a while some farmers came along. "There is Bouki sleeping on the trail," one of them said.

"No," another one said, poking Bouki with his hoe, "he must be dead."

They sat him up, but he fell down again.

"Yes," they said, "old Bouki is finished. We'll have to take him home."

They picked him up and carried him, feet first, head behind. As they walked, the donkey followed and sniffed at

Bouki's face. Bouki sneezed. When the men heard that, they dropped Bouki on the ground and ran.

Bouki lay without moving. Some other farmers came along. "Look!" they said. "Old Bouki is dead!"

They also picked him up and carried him. After a little while they stopped. "Which trail goes to Bouki's house?" one of them asked.

"That one between the trees," another one said.

And another answered, "No, it's straight ahead."

They put Bouki on the ground while they argued. "This way," one said. "That way," another said.

Finally, without opening his eyes, Bouki moved his arm slowly until it pointed back the way they had come.

"It's not proper for the dead to argue," he said. "But all of you are wrong. We passed my trail way back there."

The farmers took a quick look at Bouki and began to run. Again he was alone. No one came. He lay patiently. After a while he felt a sensation in his stomach. "If I was alive," he thought, "that would mean that I'm hungry. But as I'm dead, I must be mistaken."

After a while he opened one eye slowly. He saw his donkey nuzzling an avocado that had fallen from a tree.

"Leave it!" Bouki shouted. He jumped to his feet and snatched the avocado away from the donkey. He opened it and ate.

Then he got on his donkey and started home. "Dead or not," he said, "I need a big bowl of rice and beans."

The Donkey Driver

A FARMER was driving his loaded donkey to market one day when the animal stopped in the middle of the road and refused to walk. The farmer shouted and pushed him from behind, but the donkey would not move on. At last the man started to strike the donkey's hind legs with a stick. All this took place just outside the gate of a large house in which a rich woman lived. Hearing the commotion, the woman came out and looked over her garden wall. When she saw the man beating the donkey, she called out: "Stop! Why are you beating that helpless animal?"

The farmer answered, "Madame, this little animal may look helpless to you. But if he doesn't carry my things to market, how will they get there?"

She replied, "Perhaps so, but there is no need to beat his hind legs. Look, he has sores there from so much beating!"

The farmer said, "Madame, I respect your opinion, but I have to get to market," and he raised his stick to strike the donkey again.

The woman called out, "Stop! Don't hit him again!"

The man said, "Madame, this donkey is not yours. He is mine."

The woman said, "Here. Here are ten gourdes. I will buy the donkey's back legs."

The farmer looked at the donkey, then at the money the woman held out to him.

"Good," he said at last. He took the ten gourdes and put them in his pocket.

The woman said firmly, "Now, I want one thing made clear. Never, never let me see you hitting that donkey on the legs, because they belong to me!"

The farmer then took hold of the rope bridle and tugged until the donkey moved a little. After a while it began to walk, and the two of them went on their way to the market.

Another day the woman again heard a commotion on the road outside her gate. Looking over the wall, she saw the same man beating the same donkey again, this time on the ears.

"Stop it," she cried. "You are beating that animal again!"

The farmer said, "Madame, as you can plainly see, I am beating his ears. The back legs may belong to you, but the ears belong to me."

"Here," the woman said quickly. "Here are ten gourdes. I will buy the ears!"

The farmer scratched his head. He looked at the donkey for some time, first at the rear legs, then at the ears.

"Very well," he said at last, and he took the money.

"One thing I want made clear," the woman said. "You are never to hit that donkey's ears again. They belong to me!"

So the farmer took hold of the rope bridle, tugged, cajoled, and shouted until at last the donkey was moving once more.

Some days went by, and there was another commotion on the road by the woman's gate. This time she found the farmer hitting the animal's rump to make him go.

"Stop it at once!" she called. They talked. And when the conversation was finished, she bought the donkey's rump.

It went on this way. She bought the animal's front legs, then his nose, then his sides, until there was nothing else to buy. She was content.

But one day the commotion occurred again. The woman went to the wall and saw the same farmer striking the donkey on the legs.

She cried out, "Stop! You are beating my donkey's legs! I will call the police!"

The farmer stopped. He tipped his hat. "Madame," he said, "this donkey is mine. Your donkey is grazing in my garden. There was nothing left of him to hit. So you see, this is another donkey. Since he is mine, his legs are mine." And he whacked the donkey vigorously.

"Wait!" the woman said. She held ten gourdes across the wall. The farmer took it. He tipped his hat.

"The back legs are yours," he said. "I will be coming by again on Thursday."

The Blacksmiths

A NEW President once moved into the palace. He liked his new job. He was contented. He took a walk through his gardens. Everything was peaceful. The only sounds he heard were the voices of the tree lizards. Then suddenly, from the other side of the wall that was near the road, he heard the clang of a steel hammer: *Tao! Tao! Tao! Tao!* And after a moment's silence, from a slightly different direction beyond the wall, there came the sound of another steel hammer: *Ka-tang! Ka-tang! Ka-tang! Ka-tang!* When it stopped, the other one began again: *Tao! Tao! Tao! Tao!* Then the two of them went together: *Tao-ka-tang! Tao-ka-tang! Tao-ka-tang!*

"Who is making that terrible noise?" the President angrily asked his gardener.

"President," the gardener replied, "those are the two blacksmiths."

"Blacksmiths!" the President said. "What are blacksmiths doing outside the palace wall?"

"They worked for the old President," the gardener said. "They shod his horses and repaired his carriage."

"But the old President is gone," the President said. "They should be gone too."

"President," the gardener said, "it is this way. Those two blacksmiths are old men now. When the former President left, he wanted to reward them for their services. So he gave them the houses they lived in on the other side of the wall, and now they do iron work for the townspeople."

The President considered the matter. He went back to the palace for dinner. All through dinner he heard the steel hammers: *Tao-ka-tang! Tao-ka-tang! Tao-ka-tang!* When he woke up in the morning, it was to the sound of *Tao! Tao! Tao!* and *Ka-tang! Ka-tang! Ka-tang!* When he went into his garden, the noise was louder. When he sat on the veranda, he heard it there. When he went into his office, the clanging of the blacksmiths' hammers came through the window. There was no escape from it anywhere.

When he awoke the next morning, there it was again: *Tao-ka-tang! Tao-ka-tang! Tao-ka-tang! Tao-ka-tang!* He said, "Those two blacksmiths have to go away! Their noise is driving me crazy!"

He went out through the garden gate and walked along the wall until he came to the first blacksmith's house. There, in front of the house, the blacksmith was working noisily at his forge.

"Cousin," the President said, "what a pity you have to live in this old broken house!"

The blacksmith straightened up and looked at his house. "It isn't such a bad house, President," he answered.

"Oh, but it should be much nicer," the President said. "After a man has worked so long, he is entitled to a better place. Not here, in the middle of town, either, but somewhere else."

"I've always lived here, President," the man said. "I guess I've gotten used to it. Besides, I have no money for a new house."

"Money! Don't worry about that," the President said. "Here, take this hundred gourdes. Go get yourself another house somewhere else. Anywhere will do."

"But President, my forge will have to be rebuilt," the man said.

"Never mind that," the President said. "Build a new forge, and I will pay for it."

"Well, I have to consider my customers," the blacksmith said. "It is very convenient for them here."

"Never mind that!" the President said. "Here! Here is another fifty gourdes!"

"Thank you, President," the blacksmith said. "I will leave this house, as you say."

"By tomorrow morning!" the President said.

"Yes, President, without fail."

The President walked on. "That's half of the business," he said to himself. He came to the second blacksmith's place. He talked to him the same way, starting out with, "How good it will be to live in another house that isn't falling on your head!"

The second blacksmith thought a while, and then he answered, "But where would I go? I have no money for a new house. And besides, the other blacksmith there is my friend. I wouldn't like to move away from him."

"Never mind him," the President said. "He also is moving. Here is a hundred gourdes, and fifty more in case you lose some business."

"Very well," the second blacksmith said. "I will move."

"By tomorrow morning!" the President said.

"Yes, President, certainly, I will go," the blacksmith answered.

That night the President was happy. He could hardly sleep because of the ringing of hammers, but he knew they would be gone in the morning.

He awoke early, just before dawn. There were dogs barking, and birds chirping, but no banging and clanging. And while he was thinking about how well he had handled the whole situation, there was a sudden sound of steel on iron: *Tao! Tao! Tao! Tao!* And then there was a reply: *Ka-tang! Ka-tang! Ka-tang! Ka-tang!* And in another minute they were both going together: *Tao-ka-tang! Tao-ka-tang! Tao-ka-tang!*

The President was very angry. He jumped from bed, dressed, and rushed down to the wall. "Those blacksmiths! They made an agreement! They took my money! And they are still there!"

He went to the first house and shouted: "Stop the hammering! What is the meaning of all this?" The man at the forge turned and doffed his hat. The President went to the second shop, shouting: "I gave you money to move, so that I won't have to listen to this maddening noise! You took my money, you are still here!" He ran back and forth shouting at the two men: "I have been cheated! You both said, 'I will go,' but you didn't go!"

"No, my President," one of the blacksmiths said. "You see, we two are old friends. We didn't want to move away from one another. In fact, we didn't care about moving from this neighborhood at all. Nevertheless, we made a deal with you. We both agreed to move, even though it was an inconvenience. So we worked out a plan. My friend moved into my house over there, and I moved into his house over here. We are both men of honor. We did what we said we would do. A little change, after all, is nice. We both thank you for making it possible."

Bouki's Glasses

ONCE when Bouki was in the big city of Port-au-Prince, he noticed people reading newspapers. If there was one thing Bouki had always wanted to do, it was to sit down and read a newspaper. So when he was finished selling his yams and coconuts, he went to a store where they sold glasses.

He tried on this pair and that pair until he found a pair

that seemed just right. He bought them and then walked along the street until he found a boy selling newspapers. He bought a paper and went up the trail to his home.

Madame Bouki had dinner ready. When Bouki was finished, he took his chair and placed it near the oil lamp. He sat down and put on his new glasses. He leaned back and opened his paper. He looked at the paper a long time. He turned the pages. He turned the paper upside down. He turned it around. He turned up the lamp so there would be more light.

At last he said: "They cheated me! These glasses are no good! I can't understand a word the newspaper says!"

Charles Legoun and His Friend

THERE was a farmer named Charles Legoun. Wherever he was, he referred to his friend God. Out in the garden he said things like, "Oh God, this is your friend Charles Legoun talking. I'm planting yams and peas here. I hope you'll see to it that they grow properly." When he went to the market, he would talk right up, saying, "Papa God, your old friend Charles Legoun is here selling cotton. I guess you're going to get me a good price for all this cotton." If he was hungry, Charles Legoun said, "Well, you know me, friend God. I hope you fix things so I get a big dinner tonight." If he went fishing, he'd sit in his boat and say, "Here I am, Papa God–Charles Legoun, just in case you missed me. You can fill my net right up with fish." If he was in a shop in town, he might say, "Well, this is Charles Legoun speaking, God. Don't let this man charge me too much."

People got pretty tired of hearing Charles Legoun talk about his friend God.

One night after dark a man went to Charles Legoun's house and knocked on the door. Charles Legoun was sitting inside with his lamp on. He called out, "Who's that?"

The man said, "I'm looking for my friend Charles Legoun."

"Who is it, who is looking for Charles Legoun?" Charles Legoun answered.

"Charles Legoun knows who I am," the man said. "We have a big conversation every day."

"What's your name?" Charles Legoun demanded.

"This is Charles Legoun's friend, Papa God," the man said. Charles Legoun sat straight up.

"Papa God? What are you doing here?"

"Well, Charles Legoun has been talking to me a long time," the man answered. "He's been asking me to do this and do that. I haven't always been able to oblige him. But there's one last thing I can do for him."

"What's that?" Charles Legoun said.

"Well, Charles Legoun is getting to be a pretty old man now, and his time is about up. So I've come to take him."

Charles Legoun jumped. He pinched out the lamp flame with his fingers.

"It's a shame," he said. "You've come all this way, but Charles Legoun isn't here. Nobody's here. I'll tell him if I ever see him, but for all I know, old Charles Legoun isn't coming back at all."

The man went away.

When Charles Legoun came out of the house in the morning, he looked carefully in all directions. He told his neighbors: "In case you hear anyone asking for me and saying he's my friend, you just tell him there's been a mistake, and I'm just somebody else by the same name."

Bouki and Ti Bef

MADAME BOUKI said to Uncle Bouki one day, "When are we going to get some fresh meat to eat with our rice? It's about time you took some yams down to market to sell, and you can bring back some meat."

"Stop telling me what to do," Bouki said. "There's more than one way to get meat."

He started out for his garden, and on the trail he met Malisso, Ti Malice's boy, leading a calf to pasture. Bouki looked at the calf carefully. "Wah!" he thought. "That calf is all meat, from one end to the other!" He said to Malisso, "Good morning! What a nice calf you have there!"

"His name is Ti Bef," Malisso said.

The more he looked, the more Bouki's mouth watered.

"Where does he generally sleep at night?" Bouki asked.

"Oh, usually he sleeps on top of that hill over there," Malisso said.

When Bouki was finished with his work, he hurried home. He said to Madame Bouki, "Don't worry about the meat. I have it all figured out. Tonight I will bring home a good fat calf. His name is Ti Bef."

When it was dark, Bouki went up on the hill with his sack to find Ti Bef. But that night Malisso didn't take the calf to the hill. Instead, he took Ti Bef to the banana grove. So Bouki prowled all around the hill, but he didn't find what he was looking for. When he came home with his empty sack, his children called out: "Papa, Papa, where is Ti Bef?" Bouki scolded them and told them to keep quiet.

The next morning he saw Malisso and Ti Bef again.

"Malisso," Bouki said, "where was Ti Bef last night? I just happened to be passing over the hill, but I didn't see him there."

"Oh, last night Ti Bef didn't want to sleep on the hill," Malisso said, "so I took him over there in the banana grove. That's where he likes to sleep at night."

So that night Bouki took his sack and went to the banana grove to find Ti Bef. He looked and looked, but he couldn't find what he was looking for. That was because Malisso had taken Ti Bef to the woods. When Bouki came home, the children called out, "Papa, Papa, where is Ti Bef?" Bouki was angry. He chased them out of the house.

The next day when he saw Malisso and Ti Bef, Bouki said sweetly, "Oh, Malisso, I just happened to be at the banana grove, but I didn't see Ti Bef."

"Uncle Bouki, last night Ti Bef decided he wanted to sleep in the woods. That's where he stays now."

But when darkness came, Malisso took Ti Bef down by the spring and left him there for the night. So Bouki looked for Ti Bef in the woods, but he didn't find him.

The next morning when he saw Malisso with Ti Bef, he said, "Malisso, I happened to pass the woods last night, but Ti Bef wasn't there. Now you had better start telling me the truth. Where is Ti Bef going to sleep tonight?"

"Uncle Bouki, Ti Bef likes to change around. Tonight he is going to sleep in that cave in the mountain," Malisso said.

Night came. Bouki took his sack and went to the cave in the mountain. He listened at the entrance, and he heard little noises inside.

"Ha!" Bouki said. "This time Ti Bef is mine!"

But the cave belonged to a tiger, and Ti Bef wasn't there. Bouki crawled inside and felt around in the dark till he caught hold of the tiger. He tried to stuff the tiger into his sack. The tiger knocked Bouki down. He bit him and mauled him and scratched him. He tore Bouki's clothes half off. Bouki fled. He came back home saying, "Wah! It is terrible! Wah! I am half dead!"

Bouki's children came out of the house shouting, "Papa, Papa, where is Ti Bef?"

Bouki said: "What a terrible thing happened! That Ti Bef is a devil! He is so small and weak in the daytime, but at night he is as ferocious as a tiger! If you ever meet him anywhere, you must pay him the greatest respect!"

So it is that the people have a saying:

"Beware of Ti Malice, beware of his children too."

The King of the Animals

It is said that once the animals decided they needed a king. A gathering was called. Drummers marched from one village to another to announce the event. The message was carried in every direction. Preparations were made. A large court was made ready for dancing and celebration. Food was cooked. The animals came. There was a tremendous crowd. The tree lizard, Zandolite, was the chairman. He addressed the assemblage.

"Brothers," he said, "we need a king. In the old days we had a king, and in those times everything was in good order. Nowadays, when we have no king, there is much disorder. Every man is for himself, and there is trouble all around us. Let us select our leader."

There was noisy discussion among the animals. Then someone called out, "Let the bull be our king."

The animals talked among themselves, and at last they said, "No, the bull isn't fit to be king. He is strong, but he likes to fight. He puts his head down and threatens anyone who stands in his way."

Someone said, "Let the goat be king."

They discussed the question again, and after a while the crowd said, "No, the goat doesn't have what a king requires. He eats the leaves off the coffee plants. He stands around for hours munching, with his beard bobbing up and down. Who wants a king who is always eating?"

Someone said, "Let the ram be king."

Again they argued. When they were through discussing it, they said, "We can't have such a creature as that for our king. Every time he meets one of his kind, he wants to fight. But if he meets a large person like the bull, he is very timid and docile. No one would be able to respect him."

"Well, then, let the donkey be king," someone suggested.

"What!" the people said in disgust. "The donkey?

Should we have for a king a person who carries coffee and charcoal on his back all day? What would people think of us? We need a leader of whom we can be proud."

"Make the guinea cock king," someone said.

"With those red legs of his? With that bald head he has?"

The animals laughed loudly. "Would we want people to say, 'The king of the animals has burned his legs and lost his hair?' Oh, no, not the guinea cock."

"What about the turkey?" someone suggested.

"No, no, not the turkey. He looks too stupid."

"Let us consider the rabbit," another said.

"The rabbit? Whenever someone comes along, the rabbit has to jump out of the way. He hides in the grass. And he twitches his nose. He has no dignity."

"Well, then, let the snake be king."

"The snake?" the crowd answered. "The person who lives in a hole in the ground? If you step on him, he wriggles but never makes a sound of protest. He crawls on his belly. No, he can't be king."

"What about the horse?" someone said.

"Horse? How could we have as king a person with a bit in his mouth and a man on his back? No, no, not the horse."

Each animal whose name came up was rejected for this reason or that. At last only the dog was left.

"Let the dog be king," someone called out.

There was applause. The animals said, "Yes, let us make the dog our leader."

They crowded around him. They started the ceremony to make the dog king of the animals. The drums were drumming. Flags were waving. The food was cooking. As they dressed the dog in his royal clothes, he smelled the meat cooking over the fire nearby. It made him very hungry. His mouth watered. They wiped his face. Saliva ran out of his mouth. They wiped his face again. Suddenly, because he couldn't control himself any longer, the dog broke loose, seized the meat in his teeth, and ran away.

"Our king is gone!" everybody shouted.

Then they began to say, "No, he isn't our king. He has stolen the meat. He is a thief. How could we have a thief for our king?"

So the great gathering broke up. Everyone went home.

This is the way it was: every creature that was proposed was rejected because he was judged by his weakness. Had they been judged by their strong points rather than their weaknesses, the animals would now have a king. As it is, they do not have one.

Janot Cooks for the Emperor

In the old days, when the Emperor was alive, there was a cook in the palace at Sans Souci by the name of Janot. One day while the Emperor was eating dinner with his wife, he said: "Today I went to the top of the mountain to supervise the building of the fortress. It was very cold up there."

Janot, the cook, said, "Emperor, it's really not cold up there at all."

The Emperor replied, "Who is this who contradicts the Emperor?"

Janot said, "It is I, Janot, the cook."

The Emperor said, "Janot, when I say it is cold, it is cold."

Janot said, "Emperor, it's not so cold."

The Emperor said, "If a man had to stay up there all night without clothes or heat of any kind, he would die."

"Oh, no," Janot said, "it's really not so cold."

The Emperor became annoyed.

"Who are you to argue with the Emperor?" he said.

"Tonight you will go up there on top of the mountain and stay there without clothing or fire until dawn. If you are still alive when the sun comes up, I will give you a hundred acres of ground for your own. But if you are dead, as you certainly will be, we shall write on your tomb, 'Here lies the fool that argued with the Emperor.' "

In the evening two soldiers took Janot to the top of the mountain. They went to the highest tower of the fortress. Janot took off his clothes. "See," he said. "It's not very cold."

But when the sun went down, the wind began to blow, and the damp mists gathered around the mountain peak. Janot began to shiver. The soldiers laughed. "Why are you shaking that way?" they asked.

"Oh, I do that to keep warm," Janot said.

In a little while his jaw was trembling and his teeth were rattling together.

"Why are your teeth doing that?" the soldiers said.

"Oh, I do that because it is so quiet up here," Janot replied.

Soon tears were running from Janot's eyes because of the cold wind.

"What is happening?" the soldiers asked.

"Oh, I am just thinking of my dear dead mother," Janot answered.

Janot began slapping his sides with his hands to warm himself.

"What are you doing now?" the soldiers said.

"Oh, this is what my fighting cock does when he is feeling good," Janot said.

As the hours went by, Janot felt worse and worse. When

the sun came up at last, he was lying unconscious on his back. The soldiers put him on a horse and took him back to the palace.

"Ah," the Emperor said, "here is my stupid cook, dead as I expected."

"No, not dead," Janot said, opening his eyes. "Just resting."

"It looks to me, in any case, as though you found it was mighty cold up there," the Emperor said.

"No," Janot said. "On the contrary, it was rather warm."

The Emperor became angry.

"What did he do up there on the mountain?" he asked the soldiers.

"He shivered, he shook, he clacked his teeth, he slapped his sides, and he cried," they said.

"What else?" the Emperor demanded.

"Nothing else," Janot said. "Except that sometimes I looked down at the lights in the palace."

"Oh, now it is clear!" the Emperor said. "You were kept warm by the oil lamps and the charcoal fires in the palace! You didn't stay with the conditions! Janot, you have lost the bet."

"Emperor," Janot said, "the lights I saw were many miles away. How could they keep me warm?"

"It is finished," the Emperor said. "You didn't live by the rules. Therefore, you don't get the hundred acres of land."

That evening when it was time for dinner, the Emperor and his wife went to the palace dining room and sat at the table. When they had sat for a while, the Emperor called one of the servants and asked, "Where is the dinner?"

"Janot says it isn't cooked yet," the servant answered.

The Emperor and his wife waited. An hour went by. The Emperor called out again, "Where is the food?"

"Janot says it is still cooking," the servant said.

More time went by. The Emperor was getting more and more angry. At last he got up and went out to the kitchen. Janot was sitting patiently, waiting for the meal to be cooked. But the pot with the food in it was at one end of the room, while the charcoal fire was at the other. The food was raw and cold.

"What kind of stupidity is this!" the Emperor shouted. "How will the food ever get cooked if it isn't on the fire?"

"Be a little patient, Emperor," Janot said. "After all, the pot and the fire are only a little distance apart."

"And do you think the food will ever get cooked this way?" the Emperor shouted.

"Emperor," Janot said, "if I could be warmed by the palace lights while I was standing up there on top of the mountain, surely this fire will be able to cook the dinner!"

The Emperor was silent. Then he laughed.

"Put the pot on the fire, Janot," he said. "The hundred acres of ground are yours."

Jean Britisse, the Champion

JEAN BRITISSE said to his mother, "Mamma, I am going to Martinique to make my fortune."

His mother said to him, "Jean, that is fine. But without money how are you going to get there? You'll have to swim."

Jean Britisse went down to the wharf. He asked people where this ship was going and that ship was going. When he found one that was going to Martinique, he went aboard and hid himself under a pile of crates. The ship went out to sea. After two days, just before dawn, Jean Britisse heard the Captain say, "Men, as soon as we reach port, unload all these crates." Jean Britisse worried that he would be found. So he made his way to the back of the ship in the dark. Then, just as the sun was rising and the ship was sailing into port, he jumped into the water and began to swim.

"Captain, Captain!" he called out.

"Did I hear someone calling me?" the Captain said.

"Captain, Captain, slow the ship down and take me aboard!" Jean Britisse shouted.

The Captain looked over the stern.

"Who's that down there?" he said.

"Captain, take me aboard!" Jean Britisse called. "I'm getting a little tired!"

"Stop the ship!" the Captain shouted. "Take this man aboard!"

They stopped the ship. They hauled Jean Britisse out of the water.

"Wherever did you come from?" the Captain asked.

"Captain," Jean Britisse said, "I was going to Martinique, but I missed the boat. I jumped in the water, but I couldn't quite catch you. I've been swimming for two days and two nights, and at last I've made it."

"Do you mean to say you swam all the way from Haiti?" the Captain said.

"Yes," Jean Britisse said, "and now I can buy a ticket and ride to Martinique with you."

"Man," the Captain said, "you don't need a ticket because you are already in Martinique."

Jean Britisse went ashore with the other passengers. Everywhere he went people said, "That's Jean Britisse, the world's champion swimmer! He swam from Haiti to Martinique, and he arrived at the same time as the ship!"

Now there were some good swimmers in Martinique, but the best of them was a man named Coqui. The people went to Coqui and asked him to race against Jean Britisse. Coqui said he would race him for five hundred gourdes. The people went back to Jean Britisse and said that Coqui challenged him. Jean Britisse said he would accept the challenge but not for such a little bit of money. So the people went back again, and Coqui said he would bet one thousand gourdes. And they agreed to meet on the seashore at dawn.

When daylight came, there was a crowd at the beach. Coqui arrived in his swimming suit. When Jean Britisse arrived, he was wearing a white suit, a new Panama hat, and new shoes, and he was carrying a heavy bundle. The crowd laughed.

"Is that the way you expect to swim?" people asked him.

"Just a minute," Jean Britisse said. "I am the man who was challenged, so I can set the conditions for the race, isn't that right?"

The crowd agreed.

"Very well," Jean Britisse said. "The race is to be from here to Cuba. Coqui can swim a straight line if he wishes, but I have a few things here in this bundle that I bought for my mother, so I'd like to drop them off in Haiti. Since I wouldn't want to meet my old friends there in my swimming suit, I'll just go the way I am. I hope Coqui will bring enough food along to last for five or six days."

Coqui listened. He took off his swimming suit and put on his street clothes.

"Here's the thousand gourdes," he said. "I'm not going to race a man who wants to swim to Cuba."

When the carnival season arrived, there were wrestling matches in the town. The French wrestler Dumée LaFarge was there. He won all the matches. They were going to give him the grand prize when someone said, "Wait, he's not the champion yet. He hasn't beaten Jean Britisse."

So Dumée LaFarge challenged him.

"Very well," Jean Britisse said. "Tomorrow morning at the wrestling court." It was arranged.

Jean Britisse didn't know how to wrestle. He sat and thought for a long time. At last he figured it out. First he went to a carpenter and ordered a coffin to be made. Then he went to a brick mason and ordered a tomb to be constructed. Then he went to the parish priest. He gave him fifty gourdes and made arrangements for him to give the last sacrament.

After that, when it was dark, Jean Britisse went to the wrestling court. There were two trees standing there, side by side. Jean Britisse dug down around the trees and chopped off all the roots. Then he put back the dirt and stamped it flat and made it look natural.

When morning came, Jean Britisse went again to the wrestling court. There was a crowd. Dumée LaFarge was waiting. Dumée LaFarge took off his shirt. He took off his shoes. Jean Britisse took off his shirt. He took off his shoes.

Just then the carpenter arrived. He was carrying a new coffin on his head. On the side of the coffin was painted the name "Dumée LaFarge."

"What kind of joke is this?" Dumée LaFarge shouted.

The carpenter put the coffin down. And he said, as he had been instructed: "What must be must be."

At that moment the brick mason came along. He went up to Dumée LaFarge and said, "Where shall I build the tomb?"

"What is going on here?" Dumée LaFarge shouted. He began to sweat.

The mason shook his head and said, "What must be must be."

And then the parish priest came walking along, reading from the Scripture in Latin. He sprinkled holy water on Dumée LaFarge.

"Stop it! I am not dead!" Dumée LaFarge said. But his legs were getting weak.

"Let the wrestling begin," the people called out.

"One moment, I must warm up a little," Jean Britisse said.

First he crouched and jumped and raced around the wrestling court. He did exercises. Then he went between the two trees he had fixed. He began to push them, one in one direction, one in the other. They leaned, and the crowd watched in astonishment. Jean Britisse pushed harder. The trees started to fall. Dumée LaFarge put on his shirt and shoes. The trees crashed to the ground Dumée LaFarge put on his hat.

"Give him the prize money," Dumée LaFarge said. "I'm not going to wrestle a man who knocks down trees just for exercise."

"Wait," Jean Britisse said. "I'm not warmed up yet."

Dumée walked away. The parish priest followed him, sprinkling him with holy water. The carpenter followed, carrying the coffin. Behind him was the brick mason. Dumée LaFarge began to run. He went over the hill. It was the last time he was ever seen in Martinique.

Waiting for a Turkey

Bouki went out to work in his garden one day, and he saw a large turkey pecking at the pumpkin seeds he had planted. He became angry. He picked up a stick and chased the turkey. The turkey ran this way and that, trying to get away from Bouki's stick. In the excitement it ran straight into a tree and killed itself.

Bouki forgot to be angry. He picked up the turkey and took it home. That night the Bouki family had a fine meal of turkey and rice.

Bouki couldn't stop thinking of the way this turkey had fallen into his hands. In the morning he went back to the garden. He found a stick just like the one he had used the day before. He sat under the tree where the turkey had killed itself. He waited.

People said, "Bouki, what are you doing there?"

Bouki answered, "Waiting for a turkey to run into this tree."

He waited. Every day he went to the tree and waited for his dinner. But no turkey came. People told him,

"Bouki, God's wonders never come twice the same way." But Bouki was stubborn. He continued to wait for another turkey to run into the tree and be killed.

So it is that people say, when they see someone waiting for something that is very unlikely to happen: "Bouki is waiting for his turkey."

Some Comments on Haitian Folk Tales

THE folklore of the Haitian people—their tales, legends, *cantes fables* (a narrative form in which the story is told with the aid of interspersed songs), proverbs, sayings, and songs—is partly of Old World (Europe and Africa) origin and partly of Haitian creation. For four and a half centuries Haitians have been drawing on their own life experience to build around the lore brought to the island by Africans, Spaniards, Frenchmen, and others. The precise origins of some stories are difficult to establish, but others can be readily traced to tales told in Western Europe, the British Isles, Nigeria, Ghana, Dahomey, and other parts of West Africa. Many of the older stories have undergone considerable change in the New World, while some retain a remarkable likeness to European and African versions.

There is an almost endless repertoire of animal tales, trickster tales, stories that account for the beginning of things or the characteristics of certain animals or natural phenomena, tall tales, tales of contests between the strong and the weak, and stories in which participative singing is the most important feature.

Among many characters who appear again and again in Haitian stories are Jean Sot and Jean l'Esprit (Foolish John and Smart John, of European beginnings) and Brise Montaigne, or Break Mountains, Haiti's *enfant terrible*. Probably the most popular of the characters are Uncle Bouki and his perpetual antagonist, Ti Malice. Bouki is ineffective, boastful, sometimes greedy, continually hungry, foolish, and often gently touching. Ti Malice is quick, conniving, and ready to deceive either for an advantage or a joke. Together, Uncle Bouki and Ti Malice form a combination for plot and counterplot, usually funny, sometimes with amoral humor. Existing evidence suggests that Bouki evolved out of an original animal character. In some old tales, for example, he is a member of an all-animal cast. In some of the Creole-speaking islands of the Caribbean and in Louisiana, he has been described as having feathers. As for Ti Malice, Haitians would roughly translate the name as meaning "Mischief." But the Ti in the name could well have come from *tio*, meaning "Uncle" in Spanish. Like Uncle Bouki, Ti Malice may also have developed from an animal character. According to the Haitian scholar Jean Price-Mars, some country people refer occasionally to Ti Malice as *lapin*, the rabbit. Both Bouki and Ti Malice play roles in tales that in West Africa had only animal participants. Central to the West African stories were animal tricksters such as the hare and the spider.

The West African spider, Anansi, is a curious combination of trickster and buffoon, celebrated for his cleverness but sometimes victimized by his own stupidity. Ti Malice seems to have inherited the spider's sharp and relentless traits and his desire to outwit and take advantage of others, while Bouki seems to have inherited a disproportionate share of Anansi's stupidities and greed. In Haiti, the interplay of these personalities is considered drama, often sheer comedy.

When God appears as a character in Haitian tales, he is represented as an ultimate, benign authority but one who has moods and impulses, who can be argued with and persuaded, and who reacts in some situations much as human beings do. In "The Lizard's Big Dance," the lizard is able to carry on his big ritual celebration even though God wishes to bring it to an end. In "The Chief of the Well," God makes an unfortunate choice in his selection of a caretaker, and he has to rectify his mistake. In "Sweet Misery," God plays what we would consider a practical joke on the cat. We discern in these tales and others the easy familiarity with God that characterizes African storytelling. Among the Ashanti, for example, Nyame, the Sky God, figures in many stories featuring animals and humans. In some of these stories, God is outwitted by Anansi, the spider trickster. Among the Dahomeans, also, the supreme deity Nananbouclou sometimes is outwitted in similar fashion, though usually the other characters are demigods, all descended from Nananbouclou. One tale in this collection portrays the Afro-Haitian Nananbouclou as the supreme referee of a dispute, and it is easy to see how, as the African experience fades into the past, Nananbouclou could become simply "God."

Much Haitian lore has to do with supernatural beings and demons. Such stories are usually interesting to Haitians more for the emotional experience involved than for humor or story line.

In making selections for this book, preference was given to tales that would provide variety and demonstrate something of the scope of Haitian oral literature. Among types not included are demon stories, which for the most part have little humor, and the *cantes fables* (*contes*, as the Haitians call them), in which songs are stressed at the expense of story. Included are tales from the Bouki-Malice repertoire, animal tales, an *enfant terrible* story with a particularly humorous ending, a creation tale of apparent antiquity, a story about a descent "under the water" to the land of the dead, some tales that explain proverbs, and some vignettes, which, while not extended or fully developed stories, give a picture of what the Haitian thinks of as deliciously funny.

Like true folk tales anywhere, Haitian tales are meant to be told and dramatized rather than read. The narrator impersonates his characters, mimicks their actions, moves around, gestures, dwells on and expands elements that seem to intrigue his audience, and generally treats his performance as a production. In some regions the accomplished storyteller is called a *maît' conte*—a "story chief" or master of ceremonies—and elsewhere he is called a *samba*. While his audience is theoretically one of children, in fact it frequently includes adults. There are any number of formalized endings and beginnings for a narration. The storyteller may begin with something like: "Ladies and gentlemen, good evening. Tonight we shall have a story. It will be a story that is not too long. It will be a story that is not too short." In another convention, the storyteller begins by saying, "Crick!" to which his audience replies, "Crack!" A formula ending to a story may be some variant of: "I was there and I saw it, and Bouki gave me a kick and sent me from there to here to tell you about it." Or again: "He gave me a blow, and I have just come to my senses." Such endings have not been reproduced in this collection, as they would be distracting in the printed context.

All of these tales are based upon narrations by Haitians. In some instances the stories were taken by ear and hand, but most of them were recorded—at the start on discs, and later on tape. Among the narrators, I especially want to thank Voluska Saintville, Wilfred Beauchamps, Lydia Augustin, Libera Borderau, Jean Ravel Pintro, Télisman Charles, Maurice Morancy, and Hector Charles.

Notes on the Stories

MERISIER, STRONGER THAN THE ELEPHANTS: If the throwing of magical objects on the ground is to be regarded as the central theme, we have here a tale that goes back to classical mythology and beyond. Its wide distribution over every continent and among geographically isolated peoples suggests great antiquity. In variants known elsewhere in the West Indies, the magical objects include needles (which turn into mountains), soap (which turns into slippery hills), salt (which turns into an ocean), and other objects. In at least one West African version, the magical objects are eggs. The wari nut (or bean) that is the magical object of this Haitian tale is nonedible and is used by the "leaf doctors" of the countryside to prepare various drugs and remedies.

Apart from the flight motif, it is interesting to note the survival here of a West African story of the stealing of the queen elephant's tail. A certain chief's wife dies, and he asks his daughter's suitors how she should be buried. Each makes a different suggestion, one of them proposing that the woman be buried in the tail of the queen of elephants. This suitor then goes to seek the tail of the elephant queen, gets it, and the magic flight follows. The tale has survived virtually intact in the West Indies elsewhere than in Haiti. The Haitian variant substitutes a great drum, but most of the essential elements of the original are still present. Whereas the African tale (Ashanti) explains in its conclusion why hawks hover over fires, the Haitian tale explains (in a way that is quite African in character) why there are so many drums and drummers and why no one is buried in a drum. It further presents the proverb: "Every drum has a drummer," meaning that every man has his master, or, in a different application, that for every force there is an equal or stronger force. The name Merisier that appears in the story is that of a celebrated, almost mythological *boungan*, or Vodoun priest, who lived in the southwest of Haiti in the nineteenth century and whose name crops up in a number of old songs. The *mapou* is a tree with an enormous trunk, associated with all manner of witchcraft, and would be regarded as appropriate for a secret rendezvous of the elephants. The name of the particular tree, *Mapou Plus Grand Passé Tout*, could be translated "The *Mapou* Tree Greater Than Anything." It is to be noted, of course, that there are no elephants in Haiti, though they frequently appear in tales of African origin still told on the island. As for the possibility of using a drum for a coffin, it is not as farfetched as it might seem. Some Haitian drums stand more than six feet high and have diameters as large as two and a half or three feet.

THE CHIEF OF THE WELL: Variants of this story of the well's caretaker are known elsewhere in the West Indies, where they sometimes contain songs, as well as in

West African and American Negro lore. In this Haitian example, the *mabouya*, or ground lizard, is appointed as the original watchman. In another Haitian version it is the frog who offends, and he is punished by having his tail taken away, explaining why frogs have no tails. In this present version God plays a part that in Ashanti lore is played by Nyame, the Sky God.

BOUKI GETS WHEE-AI: Here we have Bouki, the symbol of slow thinking, and his antagonist, Ti Malice, in action. The general plot is an old one in folklore. Someone searches for something that he is led to believe is quite wonderful, only to find that it is really something quite different. In this case, of course, whee-ai is an exclamation of pain, a fact that is readily perceived by Ti Malice. Another tale in this book, "Sweet Misery," has a similar plot. The device of misunderstanding because of someone's deafness is found in folktales everywhere. This Haitian story appeared originally in Courlander, *Uncle Bouqui of Haiti*, Morrow, 1942.

BREAK MOUNTAINS: Break Mountains (Brise Montaigne) is a gargantuan character in Haitian lore who appears from time to time in stories that depict his brute strength. This episode portrays Break Mountains as an *enfant terrible* and has an almost unique humorous twist at the end. It recalls a Mende story from West Africa in which a powerful man is brought to his knees when a feather falls on his back, and a Somali story about a giant who picks up a mountain to throw at his enemy but has to set it down because of its weight when a bird alights on it.

BOUKI RENTS A HORSE: In this episode of the Bouki-Ti Malice cycle, Bouki again finds himself unequal to the situation, and he is saved from his difficulties through Ti Malice's intervention. It is understood among Haitians that Bouki is very stingy, so that the contest over the fifteen gourdes between him and the equally stingy Mr. Toussaint is laden with unspoken humor. Bouki's slow thinking is pointed up by the fact that even after the contest is decided, he is still debating whether or not Grandmother could have been gotten on the horse. The gourde—the Haitian currency—is worth twenty cents of the American dollar, and the fifteen gourdes—three dollars—is for the Haitian peasant a significant sum. In slightly different form, this story originally appeared in *Uncle Bouqui of Haiti*, previously cited.

PIERRE JEAN'S TORTOISE: The central theme of this tale—the talking or singing animal (or object) who refuses to talk when proof is required—is widespread in African and other cultures. A similar tale from Ghana also has the tortoise as the chief character. In Angola, the talking object is a skull. This variant has been found in the American Negro repertoire, and a related tale is known in Burma. A version from the region of the Congo has a talking leopard. In many of the African variants a proverb or a moral conclusion develops at the end. Here, too, in this Haitian narrative, the tale ends with a popular proverb. Another widespread theme found in the tale is that of the land animal, which is given feathers by the birds, only to have them taken away when needed. This story is based upon "The Singing Tortoise" given in Courlander, *The*

Drum and the Hoe, Life and Lore of the Haitian People, University of California Press, 1960.

THE CAT, THE DOG, AND DEATH: This tale, known in various forms elsewhere in the West Indies, echoes a story found among the Hottentots of South Africa, the Akamba people of Kenya, and elsewhere on the African continent. In the Hottentot story, the moon wished to send a message to men to tell them that as the moon dies and is regenerated, so shall it be with mankind. The moon selected the grasshopper as messenger. But the hare took over the task from the grasshopper and reversed the sense of the message, saying, "Just as I die and remain dead, so people shall die and remain dead." Since people believed the hare, they do not live again after they die.

SWEET MISERY: As mentioned earlier in these notes, "Sweet Misery" has essentially the same plot (though with different characters) as "Bouki Gets Whee-ai" and may well have been an ancestor of the Bouki tale. This story appears to have a considerable distribution through the Creole- and English-speaking islands of the Caribbean. Following as it does here "The Cat, the Dog, and Death," the fate that befalls the cat might appear to be a kind of heavenly retribution, but this sequence is accidental and the events are unrelated. "Sweet Misery" merely attempts to assign a reason for the fact that dogs always chase cats.

THE GUN, THE POT, AND THE HAT: Here, once more, Bouki demonstrates his almost infinite capacity for being outwitted by Ti Malice. Underlying all of his mistakes is his perpetual concern for food. In slightly different form, this tale appeared originally in *Uncle Bouqui of Haiti.*

THE LIZARD'S BIG DANCE: The setting of this story is the Haitian *mangé mort,* or feast for the dead—that is, for one's ancestors. While solemn in intent, the *mangé mort,* like almost all other Afro-Haitian religious ritual, involves dancing as well as food sacrifices and verbal supplication. In Afro-Haitian tradition, dancing is, in fact, one form of supplication. The *mangé mort,* which is a family occasion, may come only once in seven, eight, or more years, but when it does, it may be an affair that continues for several days. The plot of this tale—in which the saints, and finally God, succumb to the appeal of the music—is widely known in folklore with varying sets of characters. In African lore it is often the more powerful animals that are forced to dance to the music of the weaker (in some instances, a trickster hero). In an Ashanti story it is the Sky God, Nyame, who is compelled to dance. An early version of this plot is found in the Old Testament (Samuel I: 19). King Saul sends men to capture David, who is staying with the prophet Samuel. As the men arrive, they find Samuel and his followers "prophesying"—that is, in a state of religious ecstasy. The messengers are overcome by what they see, and they too begin to prophesy. At last Saul himself comes, and he also begins to prophesy before the Lord. A different version of this Haitian tale is contained in *The Drum and the Hoe,* previously cited.

BOUKI BUYS A BURRO: Bouki in action again. Here we have the Haitian treatment of "Don't count your chickens before they're hatched." The tale originally appeared in *Uncle Bouqui of Haiti.*

TICOUMBA AND THE PRESIDENT: In various guises, the plot of this story is known widely. The Old World kingly tyrant who makes the various conditions here becomes the President, and there is a unique atmosphere of Haitian tolerance for presidents, of whom there have been many. The President represents authority, but he is not too big to deal with, as the story shows, if one goes about it properly. The final episode here, the "walking on foreign soil," does not appear in any of the Old World variants that I have seen, but it has been noted elsewhere in the West Indies. It is probable that a local joke was incorporated into an old tale. In some Haitian variants the hero is given as Ti Malice and in at least one instance as Anansi. The story as given here is based on the version titled "The President Wants No More of Anansi" in *The Drum and the Hoe.*

NANANBOUCLOU AND THE PIECE OF FIRE: The characters in this tale are demigods of the Vodoun cult, and all are of African origin, primarily Dahomean and Yoruban. The story itself recalls an Ashanti tale of how the moon (or sun, in some versions) came to be in the sky instead of on earth. In the Ashanti version, the bright object is found by Anansi, and his sons argue their individual right to own it, until Nyame, the Sky God, in irritation throws it into the heavens.

THE FISHERMEN: Bouki here pits himself against Ti Malice in a fishing venture. In many of the details, the tale corresponds closely with an Ashanti story in which the spider trickster tries to outwit his partner and turns out to be the dupe. A portion of this Haitian variant originally appeared in *Uncle Bouqui of Haiti.*

WHO IS THE OLDER?: The humor of this encounter between the goat and the bull is elusive and gentle—or does it have a little sting? To a Haitian, the confrontation has immediate social connotations, as it recalls various pomposities and silly arguments between human beings.

THE VOYAGE BELOW THE WATER: In Afro-Haitian belief, some, though not all, of the spirits of the dead go to live in a place described as being "below the water." The way to this abode is the "water road"—any body of fresh water, such as a river, a waterfall, or a spring. The place "below the water" is not heaven, but simply a place where, in a different dimension, people go on much in the way that they did on earth. During special rites held by the living, the dead are believed to communicate with their descendants, usually through the mouth of a cult priest. There are numerous Haitian stories about living people who descended through springs or rivers to the place "below the water." In this particular tale there are elements indicating that it is not of recent origin. A tale recorded in Angola has an almost identical theme: A chief who has lost his wife refuses to let life go on normally in his village until his messenger descends to the place of the dead and returns with a bracelet and message from the deceased woman.

BOUKI CUTS WOOD: This is a familiar situation, with a man cutting a limb while sitting on the wrong end. The thread of this tale is found in numerous settings in Europe,

Asia, and Africa. The term *bocor* is roughly synonomous with *houngan* (which appears elsewhere in this book), both meaning the Vodoun cult priest.

THE DONKEY DRIVER: A yarn that probably developed out of a local humorous situation. The Haitian donkey, along with the human head, is an indispensable means of transporting commodities to and from the marketplace. A Haitian proverb says: "Thank God for the donkey. If it were not for him, the Haitian would have to carry everything."

THE BLACKSMITHS: Here the President is outwitted again by humble people, as a result of his failure to be more explicit. Taking him at his word and honoring their promises, the blacksmiths resolve the problem in a way the President could not forsee.

BOUKI'S GLASSES: Another joke transmuted into a tale, with Bouki assigned the role of the man who thinks all one needs to be able to read is a pair of glasses. Different forms of the joke are known throughout the West Indies. In one brief tale on this subject, the preacher, who cannot read, announces to his congregation:

> "My eyes are blind, I cannot see,
> I have not brought my specs with me."

CHARLES LEGOUN AND HIS FRIEND: This tale needs no comment. Charles Legoun is the name dropper *par excellence.*

BOUKI AND TI BEF: The proverb or saying with which this tale ends—"Beware of Ti Malice, beware of his children too"—recalls the Ashanti saying: "Nobody tells stories to Intikuma." In Ashanti lore, Intikuma is Anansi's son, and Anansi is the owner of all stories. The intent of the Ashanti saying, therefore, is that Intikuma is intimately familiar with his father's tales. This Haitian variant means that since Ti Malice is a past master at tricks, one can reasonably suppose—as the story demonstrates—that Ti Malice's children have learned a great deal from him. Tigers are of course not native to Haiti and are not found in Africa either; this actor was undoubtedly taken over from European lore.

THE KING OF THE ANIMALS: Numerous African and Afro-American stories deal with the selection of a king by the animals. Here, however, the ancient animal protagonists such as the lion, the elephant, and other creatures of the bush are noteworthy for their absence. The cast includes only those familiar to the countryside. The rabbit is a special case, being hardly known in real life in Haiti, though immortal in tales, and sometimes (as mentioned earlier) confused with Ti Malice. The story explains why, in Haiti at least, the animals have no king, and in addition it conveys the moral (and practical) idea that people should not be judged on the basis of their weaknesses but of their strengths. It recalls a similar tale in U.S. Negro lore in which the animals get together to discuss their faults. Instead, however, each animal discusses the faults of the others, and the meeting breaks up without its objective having been achieved. In the Haitian tale we have another example of the dog's inability to resist the smell of food (as in "The Cat, The Dog, and Death"). In a familiar Ashanti story, a dog wrestles all night with temptation and finally succumbs by eating the cooked meat.

JANOT COOKS FOR THE EMPEROR: This is the Haitian version of "The Fire On the Mountain" theme, which is known widely throughout the world. Other West Indian variants also have been recorded. The Haitian form of the tale seems to have specific references to the Emperor Henry Christophe, whose palace was named Sans Souci and who built a large fortress, the Citadel, on a high mountain near the town of Cape Haitian. Otherwise—except for humorous dialogue and the frivolous, offhand manner of Janot—the story seems very close to other variants.

JEAN BRITISSE, THE CHAMPION: Elements of this tale, particularly the swimming hoax, are known throughout the Caribbean. The episode of the wrestling match is encountered, as well, in the Negro folklore of the United States, although in the Haitian version certain details (such as the appearance of the carpenter with the coffin, the priest, and the brickmason) have a particular local color. The outwitting of a French champion by a Haitian trickster has special appeal to the Haitian story audience. There is a suggestion in some of the variants that the episodes presented here are fragments of a larger cycle.

WAITING FOR A TURKEY: A tale known widely in the folklore of the West Indies and other Negro communities in the New World.